WALTER
&
FLORENCE
and other stories

WALTER
&
FLORENCE

and other stories

SUSAN HILL

LONG BARN BOOKS

First published in Great Britain in 2020 by Long Barn Books
Copyright © Susan Hill, 2020

A CIP catalogue record for this book is available from the British Library.

ISBN 978-1-902421-18-6

Printed and bound on behalf of JFDi Print Services Ltd.

Contents

For
Julie Martin,
my loyal designer

ACKNOWLEDGEMENTS

The Quiet House first appeared in *The Radio Times* and *Reader, I Married Him*, in the collection of that title edited by Tracey Chevalier (published by HarperCollins).

WALTER AND FLORENCE

WALTER AND FLORENCE

1.

'That insurance man's at the door again, Flo.'

The knowing lift in her sister Ellen's tone. But Florence had already marked him from their bedroom window, coming down the street.

'Funny that.'

Norah took it up. 'Yes, funny that!'

Everyone waited for his knock on the door and everyone waited for Florence to answer it.

'Good afternoon.'

He raised his hat, as he always did. Which was only one of the reasons she liked him.

'I was just coming to check that everything was in order.' He settled his hat.

'It being the end of the month.'

'Oh, I think so. I'm sure it is. But perhaps I should just ask mother? If you'd care to wait.'

Huddled in the hall behind her, Ellen and Norah did

a mimed imitation, simpering and nodding. 'Perhaps I should just ask mother?' 'If you'd care to wait.' And clapped their hands to their giggling mouths.

This had gone on for seven months now with nothing moving forwards but Florence was happy enough. She was the eldest, she was twenty, things would come right and so she left Walter Stanway to wait on the doorstep, and went to ask if the insurance was in order and returned with her mother's kind regards and to say that it was, perfectly in order.

'I'm very pleased to hear that, Miss Hope, thank you and please give her my kind regards in return.'

He was tall and quite well set up and when he took off his hat, his hair was seen to be fair, thick at the back, but receding, revealing a broad forehead. He had taken over the insurance round from his uncle the previous year.

'I will be sure to, Mr Stanway, thank you very much.'

She had to wait to close the door until he had stepped back and turned away, because you did not close a door in someone's face, but then he raised his hat again and instead of moving, said quickly, 'I have finished for the day now, Miss Hope, I wonder if you'd care to stroll with me to the Jubilee Garden?'

Two months later, Walter Stanway was invited to Sunday

tea, which was always a sit-down meat tea, at the table and always the same, even when an uncle and aunt or cousins joined them, so everyone was taken aback at the difference. Besides Florence, Ellen and Norah, there were Hilda, Clara and Pam, plus the one remaining brother, Clive. Sidney had died of scarlet fever, John of whooping cough, aged four and thirteen months. Of the girls, only Florence remembered the brothers and she always thought that it was as though water had closed over their heads, for they were never spoken of.

No young man had ever been to Sunday tea and Sunday tea had never been a spread of these proportions, with not only cold beef but pork pie and tongue, not only bread and butter but toast with gentleman's relish, plus scones, pikelets, three kinds of cake, iced fancies and a trifle. Later, talking the whole event over in the smallest detail, Ellen accused the younger two, Norah and Pam, of having eyes out of their heads like gobstoppers and Hilda said their mother had put on the voice she only assumed for special visitors though Mrs Stanway always denied it and pinched her lips together in the gesture she used to cut short further remarks.

Florence was almost completely silent throughout the occasion, though she handed round plates and offered milk, sugar, a second slice of Battenburg. Her insides seemed to be made of wires, tangled together and pulled tight.

But Walter Stanway was at ease and carried all before him, courteous towards the parents, amusing and affable with the sisters, eating well but not a greedy amount, passing compliments on the food, listening to everyone when they spoke without ever interrupting.

It was an odd habit of the Hope family never to discuss or even refer to an event once it had taken place, not even Christmas or a significant funeral, and so, after Walter had left, accompanied by Florence as far as the railway bridge at the end of the road, it was as though he had never been inside the house and no one had ever sat down to tea. The girls had to wait until they were in bed, the older two huddled together in their room with the three young ones for half an hour, to whisper about everything and speculate, while Florence, since turning twenty, stayed downstairs with their parents until nine o'clock, reading or crocheting a lace collar or the edging for a tray cloth.

She did not catch her mother's eye, her father had gone out to the Men's Sunday Meeting, and she was happy to go over Walter's visit in every detail, the same as her sisters were doing upstairs, but silently, privately, in her own head.

She was unsure about him, not because she disliked or

had anything against him. She enjoyed his company, she laughed with him and she was sure he was trustworthy, as he was certainly steady and hard working. Was this how she should feel, was this enough, if he should propose to her? She had none of the emotions she had read and heard of, crazy passion, adoration that made you sick and the thought of those frightened her, she would not know herself and she had always done that.

But she did not know herself a month later, when she became unwell, though at first she did not take what was happening to her as illness, just as something strange and annoying. She was walking home from her work at the milliner's one warm May afternoon when she was aware of being thirsty, with a thirst she thought must be like that of people who were lost in the desert and saw mirages of water, because she started to imagine it pouring in a cool stream from the tap, filling glass after glass and herself drinking every one, impatient for the next to fill up. She began to run, and by the time she reached the house, she was almost in tears because of her thirst. She stood by the kitchen tap and did as she had imagined, and the water slaked her thirst for a few moments but then she was anxious for the next. After four full tumblers of water she felt better, and though the thirst came on again after supper that evening, and she drank more, it was not quite as urgent. But there was always a glass jug of water beside her own bed and one by Hilda's and for the first time in years, she woke and drank her own and then crept across the room for her sister's. She had to go to the lavatory several times, of course, and the same happened at work, she drank and drank and then had to leave her workbench repeatedly. People noticed, her sisters remarked. In the end, she told her mother, though as she did so she felt stupid, for how could simple thirst be of any consequence?

Neither of her parents had so much as heard of diabetes and they were terrified, but the worst thought for Florence was that Walter Stanway would want nothing more to do with her, because there was no cure, she must inject herself with insulin three times a day, and be strict about her diet and weigh her food, for the rest of her life.

She wrote him a letter saying that she felt it best for him not to see her again, and then tore the letter up and burned it, because after all they were not engaged to be married, there was not even an understanding between them, and what she had written would be a presumption, and an embarrassment to them both.

In the end, after she had been 'not at home' to all his visits and refused to open the notes he sent, he simply waited for her to leave work one day, kept behind until she parted from her two colleagues and then moved up to walk beside her. He said that he was bewildered and hurt, and asked what he had done wrong and Florence had no argument against him, could not bear the expression on his face, and his gentle tone, and then they walked on in the direction of the park and sat on a bench while she told him about her illness.

'But why do you think I would not want to know you just because of that? I don't understand.'

'Isn't it obvious?'

'Not to me.'

So that in the end, they just sat together and Florence knew that they had at last reached their understanding.

They were married on a hot day in September, with all of her sisters as bridesmaids, wearing long pastel silk with matching hats and carrying sheaves of flowers, and all she remembered was of Walter's face suffused with tenderness and pride, and her own sense that she had walked into a place not only of happiness but of safety. Or so it seemed.

Walter's parents kept a grocer's shop on the canal side of the town, where the biscuits sat in glass-lidded tin boxes and the butter was shaped with wooden paddles from a huge block into pounds and half and quarter pounds and the place was dim and smelled of tea and raisins. There had been a short, sharp falling out between them when Walter had said he would not take over the shop, ever, but wanted a different life and, as he was an only child, it seemed to them that they would be working their lives out to no purpose, and the shop became a mere drudgery and not an investment in the family future.

He had also refused to bring his wife to live there, in the house that was joined to the shop, but instead he rented one in a terrace mid way between both their families and close to the park, though the rent was high, so that he had to extend his working hours and take on many more clients, and Florence was obliged to continue at the milliner's. And so life began smoothly and they settled into the new routine and into one another, and when she looked at him, she was aware of her luck, because he was good, hard working, always anxious to please her, and never spoke an ill-tempered word.

But gradually, he came to resent the long days and the books he had to bring home and sit working at until midnight. 'You should change, you shouldn't be exhausted and not even enjoy what you do,' Florence said, and he had taken that as the permission he had not been able to give himself, and started looking for a different job.

* * *

Her illness was not a great concern because her body had adapted to the medicine well and she had got used to her diet, her tests and injections and visits to Dr Metcalfe. The only sadness was that both he and the specialist advised that she should not have children. But within the year, her sister Hilda married, the other girls would surely follow and all of them would make up, with their own, for the children Florence was not allowed to have.

It took longer than Walter had expected to find a new opportunity and he was sometimes downcast at the end of a day trudging from house to house, collecting insurance.

'Perhaps it's all I'm suited to,' he said, 'Still, I have a good head for figures and a careful hand, I should be grateful I can make use of both.'

In the end, it was a chance advertisement in the newspaper that led him to the opportunity.

'High class commercial representative required. Must be well presented and well mannered, personable and able to get on with customers, enthusiastic, hard working, with a good grasp of figures. Training will be given and a salary with commission and bonuses commensurate with results.'

'Only it doesn't say exactly what you would do,' Florence said anxiously, 'or what you would be a representative for.'

'I am going to find out.' He was never downcast for long, always determined to do well, forge ahead, look after her, and in a nicer, larger house with a good garden, though she had never asked for any of that, she was quite content.

The opportunity was to be a hosiery sales representative in the nearby city and two small towns that were fast becoming swallowed up by it. He would take the train every day, to visit stores and shops, show samples, discuss stock, listen to any complaints. Take orders. Once a month he would go to the factory office for a morning, to be briefed on new merchandise and retail changes, and discuss his sales figures.

Over tea, after she had listened to him, Florence was silent, ordering her thoughts and turning over what he had told her, for Walter was shining with enthusiasm and confidence, but she was more cautious.

'Will you not find going from shop to shop as bad as from house to house?' she said in the end.

'Every one will be different, and I will be talking to people, not standing on their doorstep waiting for them to hand over money. It will be new, Flo, it's an opportunity.'

She was touched by his faith. 'Well then, that's wonderful and I'm so pleased for you.'

'And more money. Not a lot more but commission when I do well, and I will do well, Flo. I know it.'

* * *

He did well. After six months, he had earned very good commission, he had excellent reports, he loved everything about it, even the samples, which he brought home for Florence to take out of his special leather case, and examine. Ladies stockings in so many different sizes and weights and colours. Men's socks. Children's socks. However many different styles and types of hosiery could there be in this world?

Men's sock suspenders and only around Christmas, slippers.

He went off every morning at seven to catch the same train, and was back on the one that arrived at six. Life went along on even rails.

Until the morning when she was putting on the kettle and Walter was in the bathroom above, from where she heard a crash, and after the crash a terrible silence, and stumbled upstairs to find him lying face down on the floor.

2.

The catastrophe he had suffered was referred to by his doctors as a brain storm and they talked to Florence about the effects, immediate and what might happen in the future. He was in hospital unconscious for three weeks, lying straight and still, with machines surrounding him, but the nurses said her presence was the best medicine, and that if he was to recover, it would be because he knew she was there, that she loved him and was willing him to come back. No medicine, nothing, would help, only her presence, and time.

His mother came but could not bear to see him as he was and went home to be ill herself. His father was shocked and could not think of what to say and in the end, stayed at home to look after her. Florence's sisters came when they could, brought her tempting bits of food and small gifts to cheer her up, a pretty scarf, chocolate, some strawberries in a best china bowl, a picture paper. They stayed with her and held her hand, as she held her husband's.

'You are the best of wives,' Norah said and Florence looked surprised. 'You are a saint, coming here every day to be with him when he doesn't even know it. How do you do it, Flo?'

'It's no hardship at all. How could it be? I'm his wife.'

'You must be angry sometimes. You must resent it.'

'But it isn't his fault, Norah. He didn't ask for this.'

Walter lived for the hours when he knew that she was with him, and slept to blot out the rest but after a while, he forced himself to face the truth, and work out how he could live with it and avoid despair. He was blind. There was a glimmer of greyness in the corner of his left eye, though it was not worthy of the name of light, and it came and went. Otherwise there was a blackness, across which shot random red or orange streaks, without warning or pattern and those were what he dreaded, until he got used to them, as he slowly made himself come to terms with the loss of sight. And then he started to make plans and talk to Florence about the future. He would make the best of it for them both, he said.

'But you can't work, Walter and I will need to be at home to look after you. I can't see how we will survive with neither of us earning.'

'I'll go back to my job of course. You'll see.'

He did and became legendary in the town, so that even now, so many years later, people remember him, as the man who left home as he had always done, walked to the station in the old way, though now he carried a white cane as well as his sample case, got on the train and then, once a month, on a bus to the factory office. He was still shown the new hosiery samples but now, the foreman talked him through each one and handed it to him to feel. The rest of the time, he started on his route to the stores and shops in the same order as before, and talked to the buyers, opened his case to show them the samples, which Florence had laid out as he told her, and was given the orders. Instead of writing them down he memorised them, and his memory seemed to expand and sharpen to meet the need.

At first, Florence made the journey with him, holding his arm and talking him through the route, but soon he asked to go alone, though she spoke privately to the train guards and the bus conductors and the buyers, fearing for him. There was no need. He never got lost, he made no mistakes, his day unrolled as it had always done, except for his blindness. He caught a train that arrived at six, and walked home from the station and Florence had a cup of tea ready to be poured as he came through the door. The routine after that had to be unchanging. Florence sat at the table with the order book open and dated, its fresh sheet of carbon paper beneath the page, and Walter began to retrace his day's journey in his mind, step by step by step, from the first store to the last, and to recite the orders as they had been given.

Stephenson's, 54 Dooley Street. Ladies' 30 denier stockings, tan. Two dozen pairs. 40 denier, Grey. Two dozen pairs. Men's socks, navy, grip top. Size 8 to 9. Two dozen pairs. Size Ten. One dozen pairs. Brown. Grip top. Size...

and on to 'Johnson and Coyle, 12 Mercer Street. Ladies' cotton tennis socks. White. Size...'

and so through his day, and when the break he had had for lunch came, Florence poured his next cup of tea and he had told her which café he had lunched at, one of three, depending on where he was, and what he had eaten – the two course roast of the day and pudding, with tea to follow, the ham and egg pie with salad and fruit crumble, tea,...and then they began on the afternoon.

'Gimpel Brothers, Hammond Place. Boys grey knee high woollen socks. Four dozen pairs, age 7–9. Four dozen pairs, ages 10 to 11...

When he had finished, and in the half hour before tea was ready on the table, he slept deeply in the armchair, and on waking, all of the day's orders were forgotten, sleep had erased them, so that Florence could never go back to check, there was only one chance for him to recite and her to record.

The six months were not even up before he was told that his job was secure, and for the next seventeen years, that was their routine and their life and Florence accepted it, as he did, for the miracle it was. She learned to drive a car so that she could take him out or visit their families, though the car was only for good weather and put up in the garage from October until March, but she loved it, the horizon stretched away further. They took holidays in the Yorkshire Dales and the Lake District and once, as far as Scotland and though both sets of parents died during this time, there were her sisters and their husbands and a stream of nephews and nieces. Norah was widowed young and she and her two daughters came to live two doors away, and so the days were livelier, but his working days and their evening routine never changed.

Until Norah, tapping on the back door and letting herself into the kitchen one morning, after Walter had left for the station, found Florence sitting at the table, looking pale as a moth and trying to fetch her breath.

'You never get away with diabetes' the doctor said. 'It's a time bomb, tick tick ticking.'

But Florence's heart stopped ticking that evening, after Walter had been sent for and brought all the way back by taxi. He was at sea and in distress in the corridors of the hospital, and had to be led to her bedside, but he was with her as she struggled for air, and her lungs gurgled, her throat rasped, with her and leaned over to kiss her and stroke her face and talk to her, telling her she would be sitting up and smiling any minute. But she was not.

Norah fetched him home and stayed with him until he fell asleep, though he would not go to bed, but sat in the armchair all night and woke several times, calling out for Florence.

After a few months, helped by them but most of all by his own determination, he went back to work, and gradually regained his confidence, and Norah learned to fill her sister's role and take the orders down and did her best, though she was slower and made mistakes at first. Things settled and time passed but life was a hollow thing for Walter, and after a year, he stopped work, not because he could not cope with it but because he could not face returning home to the house without Florence, he found it better not to leave it at all for very long.

He did leave it every morning, to walk to the park and sit for a while, and sometimes, people who knew him came to sit with him for company.

Norah worked now, as a dental receptionist, and so he saw less of her. The evenings were lonely but he was sent talking books and listened to history and the novels of Sir Walter Scott, the war diaries of great generals, and accounts of travel, to Asia and the Americas. Norah kept his house immaculate, and he either ate a meal she left for him, went to have supper with her or to a café in the town, where they came to know him well and would occasionally ask him what he might like cooked for another day.

But it was not only the chef and the proprietor and the waitress who knew him. He was watched by a woman who came sometimes alone, sometimes with her adult son, and sat on the opposite side of the café, spinning out cups of tea and occasionally, an iced bun between them. Perhaps they were poor.

It was at least a fortnight before they approached Walter. They sat next to him and the man knocked his white stick onto the floor.

'Dennis, look what you've done... pick that up, the gentleman will need it when he leaves.'

'Sorry.' They exchanged looks and then the man put the stick back.

'I do apologise,' she said to Walter, 'he's a great clumsy oaf sometimes, aren't you Dennis?'

'If you say so.'

'No, no need to apologise, that's perfectly all right. But thank you.'

'No trouble.'

That was all. For the time being. Walter left the café

and they sat on with their cups of tea, not speaking. Not for the time being.

She was a small woman, perhaps in her fifties, perhaps a little older, with well permed hair and a good coat. She had a pinched look about her mouth. Her hands were never still, moving between her cup and her face, adjusting the scarf round her neck, fiddling with her coat buttons, brushing an invisible bit of fluff off the man's sleeve, or tie, fidgeting with the spoon in her saucer. He was large, heavy and still, except when he ate and drank.

'We'll go in a minute, then,' she said. 'Dennis? Are you listening?'

He nodded. He was her son and he was twenty seven, he lived at home, he was not in any way handicapped or incapable, just slow, slow and lazy and happy for things to continue as they always had, with his mother waiting on him but also ordering him about in every area of his life, large and small. The husband and father was long gone. Dead, everyone supposed.

'Next week,' she said. Her name was Vera.

It was less than a week and they did not meet in the café because they took the route through the park and found Walter there, sitting on the bench.

'Go and get us a cup of tea from the kiosk,' Vera said. 'And some biscuits.'

There was a bench adjacent to Walter's. Dennis came back with two paper cups of tea.

'What sort of biscuits?'

'They had custard creams or digestives or bourbon. I got custard creams.'

'I'd have preferred bourbon. I'd expect you to know that by now.'

She glanced at Walter and saw that he was smiling slightly.

'You'd think my own son would know what biscuits I like.' She spoke in Walter's direction.

She calculated a wait of three minutes on her watch and then said, 'Excuse me… I think we met before…last week. I think this great clumsy oaf knocked your white stick onto the floor. In the Regal Café?'

'Oh. Yes. Someone did. Yes.'

'Good afternoon again.'

He hesitated. 'Good afternoon.' But turned his head away. He did not find it easy, meeting people he did not know. But she seemed to think he did know them.

'I'm Vera Pelham. This is my son, Dennis. How do you do?' She leaned over and touched his arm. 'We should shake hands, shouldn't we?'

He looked troubled for a moment, but she had guided her hand towards his.

'Dennis?'

'What?'

'Shake hands with...'

But Walter was standing up.

'Nice to have met you,' Vera said. 'I'm sorry, I don't think I know your name.'

Walter was walking away and perhaps did not hear her.

'We'll find out,' she said.

She waited several days before returning to the café twice.

'He's not here,' Dennis said. 'I knew he wouldn't be.'

'He'll be back.'

But it was over a week and this time, she was on her own and spotted Walter coming out of the stationer's shop, a paper carrier bag in his hand. Vera crossed over the road quickly.

'Good morning, we meet again. I'm Vera, we were sitting on the bench next to you in the park. I was with my son Dennis.'

She had planted herself at an angle between him and the wall so that he was forced to stay.

'I hope you're well.'

'Very well, thank you...'

'Do you mind my asking you something, though of course if it's an intrusion...'

He cleared his throat, but said nothing.

'I do admire the way you get about, in and out of shops and so on, off to the park, off to the café. I mean, with your... '

'Blindness.'

'Yes. Yes, it's better to have things straight.'

'I should be getting home ...'

'You always seem to be on your own. I mean, not to intrude but do you have a companion... a wife perhaps.'

'My wife died.'

'Oh no... How terrible for you! I knew I shouldn't have said anything. Please forgive me. I do apologise.'

He had not thought about this woman at all, who she was, how they kept meeting, not tried to imagine her, not wondered about the son who was usually with her, but now he listened to her, assessed her from the way she spoke and not the words but her tone. The woman he knew best now was Norah, he could compare their voices and so work out that Norah was younger. Norah's voice was on a level with his own face, she was of the same height, tall for a woman. This one spoke a little below that.

'I was just thinking of going to the café,' Vera said.

Somehow, he found himself going with her, sitting at the same table, explaining that they knew how he liked his coffee, agreeing to a scone though he did not usually have anything to eat.

Afterwards, he realised how much he had told her about himself, about his life, his blindness, Florence, his parents, her background, Norah and the two daughters. He had not intended to say so much and was still unsure how it had happened except that she was friendly and encouraging and persuasive. It was not that she had plied him with one question after another, she had only put one or two, and then murmured as he spoke, so that he felt drawn on. She was interested. She seemed to know some things about him before he told her though he knew it was only guesswork.

He worried about it as he made his way home but the post had brought a new set of talking books and in settling down to listen to *The Seven Pillars of Wisdom*, the woman called Vera was quickly out of mind.

His address was easily found now that she had his name. You went to the library and looked in the electoral roll and there was the whole town listed, if they were permanent residents and of voting age.

Stanway, Walter Noel 52 Crown Street.

'You don't come this time, Dennis. You can take the list and go for the groceries.'

She knew Crown Street, long with hedges and trees

spaced all the way down. It took half an hour to walk but there was a 14 bus that stopped at the end, she could get that practically from outside her own door. Still, the walk was nice.

She went slowly by, not looking at it closely the first time, but she could see it was neat, a good size, bow window at the front, bit of garden but the side had a gate and beyond that she saw more, shrubs and a small willow. There was no sign of anyone and after waiting ten minutes, she walked by again and this time, stopped at the gate.

Norah came round every morning, to tidy and clean a room, take any food she had prepared in her own house and put it in the new refrigerator, or under a plate on the table. She felt sorry for Walter, he was lost without Flo, but she had never wanted to spend much time with him, they had nothing in common, and her daughters needed her. They were twelve and fourteen now and her first priority. But she had made a pact with herself, that while he was there alone, she would look after him as she could. He could shave and bath and tidy himself, he washed up and put things away though usually in the wrong order. He went for walks every day, he listened to his talking books. In good weather, he sat in the garden. He didn't chat to her much, just the odd word, but he was always grateful, always told her he would never have managed without her. How her voice reminded him of Flo's.

A woman answered the door, which made Vera step back.

'Good morning?'

A tall woman, with hair back off her face. A closed-in sort of face.

'Mrs Sanderson?'

'No. You have the wrong house.'

'Or perhaps I have the name wrong?'

No reply.

'The blind gentleman?'

The tall woman hesitated then said, 'Mr Stanway' but as if she was imparting secret information. Her lips were narrowed so the words found it difficult to emerge.

'Of course, Mr Stanway. How silly of me. So you are Mrs Stanway?' Though Vera knew that she was not.

'No.'

'Ah... and...'

'Was there something you wanted? Mrs ...?'

'I just wondered if Mr Stanway had by any chance left his wallet in the café. I don't have it, the café has it, they found it under a table, the table I thought he'd been sitting at. They've kept the wallet, but I said I was coming by, it's on my way home, so I'd set his mind at rest or I could bring it round for him tomorrow.'

'I am quite sure he has not left his wallet anywhere.'

'I see. Well, the people in the café…'

'It must belong to someone else. Thank you for enquiring.' She started to close the door.

'Would you tell him? Just in case? You could be mistaken. So would you tell him I came to enquire?'

A flicker of uncertainty on her face, which she noted.

'I am so sorry, you must think I'm intruding and I wouldn't want that for the world. I meet Mr Stanway sometimes, we have a chat or a cup of tea… such an interesting man and I do so admire him.'

The door moved a fraction.

'It can't be easy.'

'If there's nothing else…'

'Of course not, of course, I mustn't keep you, I know I chat on too much. Goodbye Mrs…'

Vera saw Walter return not long afterwards, she saw him as she lingered further down the road, tap tap with the stick ahead of him.

'Did you go?' Dennis asked later. 'Did you see him?'

'I saw a woman.'

'What sort of woman?'

'Difficult. I shall have to think about her.'

'You will. You'll think and then you'll do.'

'We'll see. Did you get everything on the list?'

'Some new library books are on the table for you, and your tea's under a plate. It's salmon salad and new potatoes. I'll have to go now, Walter. How are you feeling?'

Walter nodded. 'Thank you, Norah, thanks for all you do. I'm getting on all right.'

He said the same thing every day and perhaps he was.

She did not mention the woman who had called, though it had not slipped her mind.

It was two weeks this time, which Dennis asked about, only to be told that rushing things was not the way but now the plan was coming together in her mind, Vera found that time dragged and she had too little to do. The kitchen was damp and the damp had caused mildew and dark patches like sweat that came through the living room wallpaper, but the landlord was deaf to the idea of anything except taking the rent money, Dennis wasn't up to much and there was no money for getting anyone in.

She went to the park when Dennis was at the library, and saw him on the bench but didn't go near. He had a paper bag with biscuits in and when he had finished eating them, he tipped the bag upside down and the sparrows and a blackbird came pecking round, though Vera thought there wasn't a lot of point as he couldn't see them. Could he see anything at all? Did even a pinprick of light get through?

Plans had to be so carefully made and even then, plans could easily go awry because of some little thing, but the little thing did not have a chance, when the stroke of luck came. She had not walked up the road, even on the other side, not knowing when the woman might be about, but one day when the bus dropped her on the corner, and it was quite early in the morning, she took a chance, and so was in time to see a taxi outside the house two doors from his and the woman and two girls on the pavement, waiting for the driver to load their suitcases. Vera shrank back against a hedge and the trunk of a laburnum tree further up.

The decision was, go now, as soon as the taxi was out of sight, or wait, take things slowly, return that afternoon? She thought it through, standing there in the sunshine, thought it through very carefully.

'Hello. I don't know if you remember me, Vera… we've met in the Regal Café? And in Prospect Park?'

It had taken him some time to answer the doorbell.

'Oh. Yes. Good morning… you are sometimes with…'

'My son. Dennis. But not today.'

'How did you find me?'

'Well that's the funny part, I didn't ... that's to say, it's a bit more of a coincidence, if you see what I mean.'

'I see, yes. Or no.' And he gave an uncertain laugh. Even on his home ground, she saw that he lacked confidence.

'I was in the café yesterday and I found a wallet under the table... and the waitress said she was sure it was yours... she looked inside and I said if there was an address I would bring it round to you, for safety.'

'That's very kind of you... but I don't think...'

'Only she didn't want to trust me with it, which is perfectly fair, even though I am a regular, she does know me, but all right, I said it would have to wait till you were next in, though who knows when that would be and you might need your wallet in the meantime.'

'I don't...'

'So I gave up at that point, but then, as fate would have it, I was getting off my bus on the corner when I saw you coming down this road, and I would have run to catch you up only my ankle isn't steady, but luckily, I saw you turn in here. I couldn't follow you yesterday, I had to get home to let Dennis in, he'd left his door key on the kitchen table that morning...he's quite forgetful I'm afraid, good boy though he is. Oh dear. I'm out of breath. Oh dear...'

'Are you feeling ill? I should... please come in, you can sit down. Is there...'

There was a hard wooden chair in the hall. 'Oh dear. I'm sorry, I'm just a bit breathless... I get like this, it's nothing to worry about. The doctor was very reassuring, said not to push myself, to rest when it happens and I'll be fine.'

He stood over her looking helpless. Embarassed even. But she thought she saw concern on his face too though it was always difficult, because you read so much into people's eyes and his were just blank, you would never be sure what he was feeling. Or thinking.

'Would you like a glass of water?'

She caught her breath several times and made her throat rasp. 'Thank you... if you don't mind...'

He went into the room on the left, making his way with care, feeling for the doorpost.

'I shouldn't make you fetch and carry, I can come in and get it.'

The kitchen was clean, without any clutter, no food or crockery left about. A clock on the wall. A bright red washing up bowl upturned against the taps. A spotless gas cooker. It was as though no one ever used it.

The window overlooked a small garden with a trellis up which a clematis scrambled. No flowerbeds, no bushes, just mown grass.

'You've a lovely garden,' she said.

He stood holding out the glass of water to her, but she had moved to look out of the window, he was holding it out to an empty space.

'You're so kind, thank you. I feel better just for stopping. This is such a nice kitchen. You keep things beautifully.'

'I don't. Not really. Norah does most things…'

'Your wife? Oh, I am so sorry, you told me your wife had died, how stupid of me.'

'Norah is her sister… my sister in law. She lives next door. With my two nieces. She's a widow. She looks out for me but… nothing more. Please understand.'

'But I wouldn't dream… I'm only pleased you're not entirely on your own.'

'In fact she – they – just went away. They'll be away for just over two weeks. I'll be a bit lost without Norah.'

'I can see that. This is very reviving and refreshing… the water.'

'It's water. I mean, from the tap.'

'It tastes better than mine, that I do know.'

'Perhaps because you were in need of it. You sound better now.'

'I am. And I won't trouble you a moment longer, I feel fine. But thank you so much, so much, I'm delighted

I found you. I hadn't seen you about … not as much. I must get home, Dennis will be waiting.'

'And he forgot his key'

'How clever of you, yes, he did. So I have to dash.'

'Don't. No dashing please, you'll be short of breath again.'

'And no knight in shining armour to take me in and provide cool water.'

Vera touched his arm quickly. 'I'll see myself out, please don't come to the door. And thank you again.'

She slipped out and up the path and was gone. He heard no sound.

'Dennis?' she started talking before she was in through the front door. 'Dennis.'

She went into the back room and switched the television off. 'Mother! What did you have to do that for?'

'Listen to me. Ouff.' She sat down suddenly. 'I'm out of breath, I nearly ran all the way up the road.'

'What happened?'

'That woman. The one who came to his door and was rude to me. It's his sister in law, she has two daughters, and I saw them all going off with suitcases. In a taxi. He said they're away for two weeks.'

'When did he say that?'

'When I ...never mind, the point is, this is my chance and I'm taking it. So you listen to me.'

'Can we have tea first?'

'No. You can go for fish and chips. This is more important.'

Not the following day, she left it until the one after, and then went and Dennis came with her, standing behind her at the front door, six feet one and burly. Not that Walter could see him but there was always a sense of his own size and bulk about Dennis. He loomed with it.

'Hello?'

'Mr Stanway – Walter... it's me, Vera. Hello. I just wanted to bring you these. You said you were having to fend for yourself and I'm sure you're very capable but there's nothing like something home made by someone else is there? Now it's... I wonder, could we come in just for a moment, only I've got the things in a bag but I need to set them down...'

He only hesitated for a second.

'I've got my son with me. You remember Dennis I'm sure.'

Dennis put out his hand, thrusting it almost into Walter's and then stepping closer to him. 'Yes. I... please come into the kitchen. This is very kind of you. You really didn't have to...'

'It's no bother. Dennis, can you hold the door open?'

She set the bag on the table and brought out a dish and a lidded tin. 'This is a cottage pie, I made it for us and I thought an extra one ... you just heat it up. What kind of an oven do you have?'

'It's gas,' Dennis said, looking round.

'Fine, so you want it half turned up and twenty minutes. Will you be able to manage, I wouldn't want you burning yourself.'

'I can do the oven, Norah's given me a lot of lessons. I manage very well.'

'Oh yes, your sister Norah.'

'In law. Sister in law. Florence – my wife – her sister. One of her sisters.'

'There's more than one then?'

'Four.'

Vera looked at Dennis who was inspecting the refrigerator.

'And in this tin here – you just take the lid off – there are two sorts of cake – almond slices and a small chocolate ... the chocolate's square and I've cut it for you. But mind you replace the lid or they'll go stale.'

'Or the mice will get them,' Dennis said. Walter looked round in the direction of his voice. 'I don't have mice.'

'How do you know? Very clever cunning little things, mice.'

'I don't have any.'

'If you want someone to kill them for you, you tell me.'

Walter stepped abruptly back.

'This is very kind of you, I'm not sure I should take them. I don't like to …'

'It's no trouble, as I said, and I was a bit worried about you, fending for yourself. I said to Dennis. Now, the other thing – I'm sure you're fit and capable but there are some jobs Dennis could do for you – help you with. The dustbins, the coal, that sort of thing.'

'I'm strong,' Dennis said. He was opening the door of a wall cupboard.

'I can manage all of that. But thank you. I… I was actually just going out, I have an appointment.'

'Well, don't let us keep you. Where is your appointment? In town? We're going into town, we can take you.'

'No. Just in The Crescent.'

'We can go that way, we'll walk you along.'

'I don't need…'

'Nice to have company.' Dennis said.

'You get yourself ready, put your coat on and we'll wait here.'

'Can I use your cloakroom?' Dennis said. 'You don't need to show me, I'll find it. I expect it's off the hall.'

Walter stood in the middle of the kitchen, isolated, as if someone had drawn a chalk circle round him. He turned this way and that. He felt uneasy, his sense of himself and his own familiar surroundings disturbed.

He did not know quite how to say he preferred to walk to the doctor's surgery on his own, so they went with him, and she took his arm, which he hated. He needed to feel his way forwards with his stick, without any other assistance, but he did not know how to say that either.

'Well, this is where we go onwards,' she said. 'Now can you manage, will you be all right? I can easily come with you to wherever you're going, Dennis and I can.'

'Thank you, no, you're very kind but I like to manage on my own.'

'I admire your independence. It can't be easy. Oh and I'll call back for my dishes... it won't be tomorrow, probably Wednesday.'

He did not want her to call back but he could not say this, either.

She arrived without Dennis, at ten on Wednesday and when Walter opened the door, she went straight in and through to the kitchen.

'I've brought you a home made pasty and a lemon

tart. I'm famous for my lemon tart. Would you like me
to put the kettle on?'

Walter had been working out what to say ever since
he had gone to bed the previous night, and not slept well
as a result. He wanted to tell the woman that he would
rather she didn't bring him food, that the pie had been
very nice but that now she should take her dishes and
leave and not return.

'I'll put the pie in the refrigerator and there's a clean
tea cloth over the tart. You can eat that cold or warm
it. We like it cold but it's up to you. Now, where do you
keep your cleaning things? This kitchen floor ought to be
mopped and the surfaces wiped down and then I can give
your living room and stairs a quick vacuum.'

'No. No thank you. Norah ...'

'But she's gone away. You can't have the house left
for over two weeks. I'm surprised she didn't arrange
something.'

'It's...'

'Cleaning things under the stairs?'

"Dennis, I want you to go round there. The linoleum
under the kitchen doorway is a bit loose, you could take
your tools – well, hammer and tacks, and fix it. See if
anything else easy like that wants doing and have a look
at the locks. Is it just an ordinary Yale?'

* * *

'I didn't know there was anything wrong with the linoleum.'

'You could measure your length on that. Mother said to come and fix it. Make it safe. I'll just do that then.'

Walter sensed the man's height and bulk, felt his body heat and his breath quite close to him.

'Yes, well, thank you, but there's really no need. Still, you could take the dishes back with you, save the bother.'

'It'll be no bother for her.'

'I might not be here though, I wouldn't want he to have a wasted journey.'

'She won't. If you're not in she'll just keep coming back until you are. What are those?'

'I'm sorry?'

'On that table. Boxes.'

'Oh. Yes. Talking Books. They send them to me like that.'

'Look a bit boring.'

'They're not boring at all'

'You could get something saucy.'

'Please don't move them, please put them down exactly where they were.'

Dennis moved them. 'Sure,' he said. He took his time with the linoleum, as he always did with jobs, because he wasn't very handy.

'That's a lot better.'

'Thank you, and please take the dishes with you.'

'More than my life's worth. See you soon.'

He would have gone out to the café but he was afraid of meeting them and so he settled into his chair and reached out to switch on the recorder,. The talking books were beside it, taken carefully out in the order they had been in their box. The machine did not make its usual faint hum and when his hand reached out and he felt all round the table, it did not touch the boxes. He got up and stumbled about until he found them and brought them back to the table but the machine was dead. Dennis had unplugged it from the wall socket, which Norah would soon have discovered. But Norah was not here. He switched on the radio and listened to a programme about shoe making followed by half an hour of light music and after that, he went out. The café was full of people having lunch so there was no free table. He left and started off towards the park, before thinking better of it and returning home.

'It's me. She's sent me to do your bins,' Dennis said. He had found the way to the side door and banged on it, giving Walter a serious fright. The side door led from the passage into the kitchen and was locked.

'I need to get your kitchen bin and that.'

'I don't need you to help me. I can do the bins, thank you.'

'No, I have to, I daren't go home if I haven't.'

In the end, it was easier just to open the door.

'How do you know this is the day for them?'

'Worked it out. Is this all your kitchen waste?'

Was it? The bins clattered and then he was back in the house, walking away.

' Excuse me...where are you going?'

'Upstairs rubbish.'

'There isn't...'

The heavy feet on the stairs and then across the room above. Walter wanted to cry at his own helplessness.

'Good job I went, there's all this waste paper.'

'What...'

'In the basket.'

'Please don't...'

The bin lid again.

'That's everything. Can I put the kettle on for you?'

'No!'

'Keep your hair on. OK, I'll go back and report. Cheers.'

What did he mean, report?

'Got the spare key. Hanging on a hook by the stove.

Honestly, people ask for burglars.'

'Hand it over. Did you see anything?'

'Couldn't be long. Nice back bedroom over the garden. He's in it at the moment. Bigger one but it's on the street. And a bit of a surprise is another staircase up to sort of dormer room, in like, the loft.'

'Just right then. Nothing lying around?'

'Didn't look. Don't want him wondering.'

Two days went by and he was alone, no one knocked on the door. It was quiet and peaceful and he had a phone call from Norah, who said they might stay away another week, if he was all right with that.

'But if you're not managing, Walter, if you'd rather not, I'll come back as arranged, you've only to say.'

'Of course you must stay on. You deserve a good holiday.'

'Well if you're sure. Is everything all right there?'

'Everything's fine, Norah. Why ever wouldn't it be?'

On the Saturday morning, he was woken by sounds below, sounds he could not identify – crockery being put down? Cutlery. The kettle whistling. He must be going mad. His hearing had grown steadily more acute over all years since his brainstorm, as well as that extra sense he had of things around him, their size and shape and placing. Distances between them. But it still took him a long time to get up and washed, shaved, dressed and downstairs, because he was only confident when he did everything in order.

He smelled frying bacon.

'Helloooo… surprise for you! It's all ready, just come and sit down. Bacon and egg, toast and tea and I found a nice pot of honey in the cupboard. I didn't know you liked honey, I must remember that.'

He felt the energy and the life and the fight drain out of him and he sat down at the table in a limp state of hopelessness, saying nothing, just feeling for his knife and fork. The son was next to him, he could feel his breadth and heaviness and warmth. 'Morning,' he said.

Walter could not summon up the strength to reply.

'That's rude,' Dennis said.

It took less than a week. They had already given notice at the flat and there wasn't very much to pack, aside from clothes and bits and pieces and they brought all those together in a taxi.

Walter was out when they arrived and she had carried up their things and put them away, worked out how the rooms could be changed around, in another week or so.

Dennis liked the room up the loft staircase, he was a king in his own space.

Vera had bought a pie at the bakers and there was a tin of peas. She didn't intend to do quite so much cooking now, he could live as they lived.

When Walter returned, Dennis had the radio on to loud dance music. She was in the back sitting room, looking in the bureau drawers and pigeon holes, finding out everything. They would be all right, she could tell that after five minutes.

Walter had given in completely, because he could not think what else to do and if he tried to struggle he knew they would win. And perhaps things could be worse, he would have someone to cook and clean and do the jobs about the house, and he had his own inner life. She could not touch that, or his past or his memories.

Besides, Norah would be back in nine days.

'Would you like a cup of tea?' They could sit round the kitchen table. He would make an effort. She had probably brought a cake.

There was no cake. No tea. 'We don't have tea just for the sake of it,' she said. 'We do things at the proper time.'

The next day he heard things being moved about upstairs and dared not go there and later, found his clothes moved to the room at the front, where there was a washbasin.

'You don't need the bathroom, Dennis and I can share that.'

He sat on the upright chair in the window and thought about Florence and the idea of her having been pushed out of what had been her bedroom, their room, made him sob, but silently, inside. But after a while, he got up and went across the landing and shouted.

'This is not right, get out of there.' The door opened.

'I won't be spoken to like that, and all when we're trying to look after you and sort your life out without any thanks.'

'I don't want you. I don't want either of you and get out of that room.'

'Dennis… will you come down here a minute.'

But he was there already, Walter sensed him, padding down the loft staircase in bare feet, like a huge animal.

'That was where Florence…'

'And it would be best if you didn't go on about Florence, better not to talk about her any more and you'll soon forget.'

He blundered his way back to the new, small front room and sat on the bed and thought nothing and felt nothing because that was the only way he could deal with it.

* * *

Norah was back three days before she had planned because Eileen was ill and so her attention was taken up with their return and sickness and medicine and doctors, she didn't have a moment for Walter until the following evening... The lights were on upstairs and down, even in the attic room, which was not usual and she was calling out his name as she put her key to the lock.

It did not turn and after three tries she banged hard.

'Oh.'

'We don't take religious leaflets or give money on the doorstep.'

'Excuse me... I don't know who you are but this is my brother in law's house, Walter Stanway, and I want to see him.'

'He's busy.'

'Listen to me – who are you? If he has employed you to look after things while I've been away that's his business but I'm back now, thank you. I can't understand why my key wouldn't work. *Who are you?*'

A very tall broad man loomed behind the woman, blocking out Norah's view of the hallway and stairs.

'He doesn't want visitors, he's perfectly happy. Now if you wouldn't mind...'

'But I do mind, I want to know what's going on and I want to see Walter.'

But the man had come forward, moved the woman aside and shut the door in Norah's face.

She went round to the window and peered in through cupped hands. The front room was empty so she went round to the back and there was Walter, in his chair, doing nothing, staring ahead, looking down at his hands. Norah tapped the pane but of course he could not see her and then the woman was there waving at her to go away and the young man started towards the side door. Norah fled.

For the next fortnight she tried to see Walter, hung about waiting to catch him when he went out. But he did not go out. She tried telephoning but the woman answered each time. In the end she went to the police who said they would go by but that people were entitled to change their door locks and have whoever they wanted to stay and unless there was any disturbance or something appeared suspicious, they had no right to intervene.

'I'd just leave it, Madam, get on with your own life, that's what I would do. All right, keep a weather eye if you feel you should, but otherwise...'

Vera asked Walter to give her money, and she went into town, leaving Dennis behind. She ordered new curtains, a new rug for her bedroom, some kitchen things, and when she returned asked Walter to give her authority to sign his cheques.

'I can't. It has to be done at the bank.'

'Then we're going to the bank.'

Dennis came with them, and although the Head Teller knew Walter well, as he had known Florence, and asked one or two questions and expressed some concern, Walter nodded and signed, with Vera and Dennis close to him on either side, and there was nothing the man could do, though he called after Walter, as they left. 'Mr Stanway, might I just have a word in private?'

But Walter was already being led out.

Vera looked through every piece of paper, every business letter and form, every passbook and statement and insurance certificate.

'Right, it's well worth it. It's over a hundred thousand.'

'Mum, you're not going to kill him?'

'Of course I'm not going to kill him, what do you take me for and where would be the point of it?'

'What are you going to do then?'

'You'll see. I'm in no rush.'

Norah could see a little way into the kitchen and back sitting room, when the lights were on. Walter was always in his chair, hunched forwards, head down, like a sagging stuffed doll. He never went out, and Vera or Dennis always went separately, not leaving him alone, until one afternoon, the front door closed and they were walking quickly up the path and away. She waited ten minutes, then went to the back door and tapped. Nothing. But then, something, a moving shadow. She heard odd sounds.

'Walter? Come to the door, I need to see you, I need to talk to you. Walter?'

The shadow moved again but that was all. Norah went to the window.

He was on his hands and knees near the cooker, a pail beside him, a cloth in his hand, hopelessly swirling it round the linoleum floor, reaching for the pail and wringing it out clumsily, spreading grey suds to and fro again. Norah let out a strange little cry.

'Madam, I appreciate your concern, I honestly do and it sounds a very strange business, and harsh, as you say, making a blind man who has never had to look after himself, wash a floor, and… well, whatever else, but it's hardly a crime is it? What do you think we could do – what would we have any cause to enquire about? We are the police force.'

It was over a month later that Norah's doorbell rang

and she opened it to find Walter standing on the step. He looked thinner, older, he was grey, his face was the face of a man who was beyond everything but the daily business of enduring. There was no fight or resistance in him.

'I can't come in,' he said. 'I've been told not to. I've been told to tell you that I'm not to speak to you again, after today but I am to tell you that on Saturday next, I have to get married. There's nothing to be done, Norah but I said wanted – I had to, say this to your face and it was agreed.'

'Oh, dear God, Walter, I can't... Walter, listen to me...' And she took him by the shoulders and half shook him, in her distress and anger. 'Walter, don't give in to this, don't agree. Do not let this happen. Get rid of them, or come here, now, come in and stay and I'll look after you, you need never go back into that house again until they've gone.'

'You don't understand, Norah. It's all been done and too late, everything's been taken over but if we are married, it will be hers, hers and his and that's an end. I don't care about it any more, Norah.'

'Listen to me, Walter Stanway, if my sister, your wife...'

'Please, no. Please, I can't talk about Florence, I can't think about her and I never mention her name out loud. But I did have my thoughts and memories, at least. Not now. I can't bear them. I try not to think about her. You think of her for me, Norah, will you? I want you to do that, please… '

'Walter, you're to stay in here and I'll shut and lock the door.'

'He'll break the door down.'

'He will not.' But she knew that he might.

A taxi came and Vera walked out to it, wearing a new looking pale blue coat and hat, with a corsage, Dennis behind in a suit that was too small, Walter, with a small buttonhole and his white stick with Dennis's hand on his arm, guiding him ahead and into the cab. Norah watched out of the upstairs window and wept. Walter could not see her.

She prayed for him to die, because it was all she could think of that would release him, but a year later and then two, and he was still there, sometimes glimpsed through the window, on his hands and knees, or at the sink with sleeves rolled up. If she could have seen further she could have watched him struggling to strip beds and make them and wipe taps and bend over the bath and scour the lavatory. He did not go out. They never left him, he was never alone in the house again and after a time, even Norah went, unable to bear living there any longer, and taking the chance of moving out when

Eleanor married a farmer and there was a cottage free. It was small, damp and dark and too near the cows and their flies but she made the best of it and so did not find out how her brother-in-law's life went on, only kept her promise to remember Florence for him, and was grateful that her sister did not know about the way Vera and her son had so cleverly carved their own comfortable future out of his. She could not know that Walter spoke to Florence sometimes now, in silent despair, begging her for help while knowing that she could never give it.

One Saturday morning, when he had not come down by nine o'clock, Vera sent her son to kick him out of bed, heard him shout down that there was something wrong and went up to find Walter dead. She had no feeling other than a mild sense of satisfaction, though when Dennis yelled out 'Hurrah' she clipped him across the face. 'You show a bit of respect.'

Dennis laughed.

The funeral was quickly over but at the end of that day, Vera felt a sourness inside her, and there was something oddly flat about the atmosphere in the house that was now hers. She had triumphed but she seemed unable to exult in it.

The days and weeks and months took on a different routine, and Dennis scrubbed the floors and washed the pots and put out the bins and swept the side path and resentment rumbled away inside him.

She had cleared all of Walter's own personal things though she kept the paperwork as he had left it in the bureau, but after a while, and in a sudden burst of energy and resolve, she decided to get rid of the last traces, other than furniture, which she felt was impersonal as well as useful. Florence's photograph was still on the sideboard but turned face down, with a small silver shield she had won at school beside it. Once or twice she had caught Walter touching or gently running his hand over them and letting it linger, before she had raised her voice. She went across and picked up the photo frame, but dropped it on the floor with a sharp cry, because she felt as if her hand had been scorched, the touch had been like the red hot plate of an iron.

She reached down but her hand burned as it neared the photograph.

A few days later she told Dennis to get the outdoor broom from the passageway and clear the mess of leaves that had fallen from the overhanging tree next door, before it rained and she slipped. But it was the broom that slipped, out of his hand, to fall sideways against an old waterproof that hung there and the waterproof also dropped down, and with it Walter's white stick.

'What in heaven's name are you playing at out there, Dennis, clumsy oaf, for...'

But Dennis was jumping about and shaking his hand and when his mother looked, she saw that it was bright red, with white wheals scored across the palm, and swelling until it was twice its size. Dennis went on shouting in pain staring and staring at it.

The cane and the picture, the waterproof and the broom went on a bonfire they made in the back garden the following night, which was calm and clear and very still. The trees did not stir. But as the fire caught, a wind came out of nowhere, swirling through the flames and great plumes of black, sulphurous smoke billowed up and spread greasy, stinking soots all over the garden, which smeared the windows and the path and thickened into a dark sludge as they fell. Only the neighbouring houses were not affected, the smoke, and soots, even the smell, did not seem to go anywhere near them.

A pair of brass letter scales stood on top of the bureau, with a tower of small weights rising up from largest to the tiniest, weights that Walter had sometimes taken off and re-arranged and put back in order again, by feel, when no one else was about.

Vera wondered if those, along with an inlaid sewing box on frail looking legs, and a small set of ivory monkeys, were of much value.

'Take them to that shop on Ainty Street,' Dennis had said. 'Sell them.'

She wondered again now, looking at the scales, but as she looked, the side with the brass pan on which letters would be placed, began to move. The scale sank down and stopped. Went still. Then rose again. Started to go down. Back.

She held her breath and stared at them and perhaps there was something wrong with her eyes, for they remained as they were for the whole time she was watching them.

As she went out of the room, the ivory monkeys moved an inch or two forwards along the mantelpiece.

When she came down the next morning, she felt that something was different, wrong, out of place but the scales were level as they always had been and she did not notice that the monkeys had moved to the other side, any more than, at least at first, she noticed a gap where an upright chair had been, set against the wall. It was only later, when a different chair, an oak ladder back with a ruby velvet seat she did not recognise, was seen to be standing in its place, that she screamed at Dennis to stop playing stupid games.

She went upstairs to bed nights later and saw that the curtains in her bedroom had been replaced. The bright blue taffetta ones she had picked out were in a tumbled heap on the floor and heavy rose-patterned chintz, faded at the corners, hung from the rail, below a pelmet where no pelmet had been that morning.

One by one, pieces of furniture, ornaments, vases, crockery, the hall clock, disappeared and different ones were in their place though sometimes, nothing was left save an ugly gap or a faded outline where a picture had hung.

Slowly, relentlessly, the house was emptied and re-furnished, and Vera understood that it would not be long before it was exactly as it had been when she had first stepped inside it, the way Walter and Florence had had it. They were taking it back.

Dennis spent most of his time in his bedroom, sitting on the rug with his back against the door, the window latched and the curtain drawn. From time to time, he whimpered.

She found a box of ladies hosiery on the doormat, Stockings, Size 5, Lisle, Dark Grey. 1 dozen. A chit for three yards of stiffened white millinery ribbon appeared pinned to the door. Walter's white stick was back in the hall where it used to be and sometimes, late in the afternoon, as autumn came on, with early dark, Vera heard it come, tap tap tap tap tap up the front path. A key would turn in the lock.

Sometimes, the sound of a man's voice, reading terrible passages from a dark book about the jungle sounded through the house, growing louder and louder as the story intensified, until Vera put her hands to her ears, and fled, leaving Dennis hunched forwards with his head on his knees, as the voice came to him through a chink in the door frame. He whimpered and closed his eyes tightly. But there was no need, because he could see nothing. Nothing at all.

THE QUIET HOUSE

THE QUIET HOUSE

The winter sun was setting but there was just enough light left for me to read the name on the gate. *The Quiet House*.

The agent had told me that nobody had lived here since the owner's death but the family, not wanting to sell it, had done some refurbishing to make it, as he said, 'Not luxurious but quite comfortable.'

I hoped that it was also warm because as I stood looking at it, the darkness closed in and it was clear there would be a hard frost. I got my bags out of the car and went inside.

My name is Jonathan Fenn and until recently I was a barrister in a London chambers but, after my beloved wife Mary died, I struggled for many months to make any sense of my work and of life in general and I had something of a breakdown. We had no children, which was only a sadness to my wife, for I have never much cared for them. Now, I longed for them, as adult men and women who were close to me. I felt desperately lonely.

It was the day before Christmas Eve. The previous year, I had been welcomed by kind friends to their family hearth and festivities, but I had felt out of place and sharing in the jollity had been hard, so I had decided early to come far away from London and spend this holiday alone. I was recovered in health and to some extent in spirits but I still missed Mary more than I can say and would not have been merry company for anyone.

I had a car full of food, wine and books, stout walking boots and warm outer clothing and I planned to make the most of the country peace.

I opened the front door. A porch gave onto a wood panelled hall, with a broad staircase ahead. I switched on the lights and went round the house. The kitchen had a range that had been lit for my arrival, a larder containing fresh milk, bread, cold beef and a meat pie under cloths. There was also a small iced Christmas cake. On the mantel I found a card decorated with a jolly robin in snow, with a message. 'Compliments of the season from G and J Murdoch. Old Harrow by Garnforth. Tel. 2399 if required.' I knew that the village where the housekeepers lived was some five miles distant, with only a farm, fields and woods between.

Moments later, as I explored two large and rather bleak sitting rooms, and one cosy snug, in which a fire had been laid, I felt the energy drain out of me. I heated the pie, opened a bottle of red wine, and after enjoying substantial helpings of both, made myself comfortable in a deep armchair beside the hearth. At first, the wood crackled and blazed but once it had settled, I felt the silence like a shroud around me. I was used to traffic, street sounds, voices, the movements of neighbours above. I had forced myself to become more sociable lately, going to my club, films, the theatre, I chaired the occasional parish committee. The country silence pressed in, I felt melancholy and fresh grief at the absence of Mary. Had I been out of my mind to come here, and at Christmas of all times? At least in London there might have been carol singers below my windows.

I went to bed at nine-thirty and lay reading, and to my surprise, I began to find the silence comforting, like a soft quilt wrapping me round. I had left the curtains half open and when I switched off the lamp, I could see a night sky such as one only dreams of in the city, ink-black and pricked all over with stars, the milky way a translucent drift.

I slept deeply but woke in the early hours, seeming to hear faint scratching sounds behind the wainscot. Mice.

I smiled, for I quite like the small, furry beasties living their secret lives.

When I woke again, it was just light and this time it was voices I heard, tiny, whispering voices. I sat up quickly. Nothing.

I had to get out. The village must have an inn, a shop, anywhere in which I would find human activity and I went out into the raw morning, noticing how overcast the sky was, with a strange yellow-grey cloud bank forming to the west. I walked from home in Hampstead down to the city several times a week, so I made short work of the tramp today, to find the village shop open. There was nothing I really needed but I bought more bread, cheese and some home-made mince pies.

'You'll be at the Quiet House.' It was not a question.

'Yes. I needed to get out of London. Who used to live there?'

She gave me a sharp look. 'Old Grace Keeley.'

'But it's a big house.'

'It needed to be, once upon a time.'

'When was that? I like country stories.'

'There were children.'

I waited, as she rang up my purchases.

'My grandmother died at a hundred and two years old. She remembered. There was a mortal illness all round the district, it took off the younger men and women, strong and hearty, not the old folk, as you'd expect. And not the children. There were so many left without parents. People did what they could, took some in but the rest were homed together...'

'An orphanage.'

'Gran always said they were half starved and cold, the Quiet House children. Well,' she turned away. 'A Happy Christmas to you. Open again Thursday.'

On my return, I went into the garden but it was empty and dull, just a lawn and shrubs. I dozed before the fire and woke to an intense hush. Looking out, I saw that there was already a covering of snow on the ground and the sky swirled with goose-down flakes. I was about to turn away when something caught my eye. Where there had been nothing on the lawn, now there was a group of eight children's chairs, together with a wooden schoolroom bench, facing one another in a half circle. I had noted a lilac tree but not the swing hanging from it, a simple plank and two ropes. No one was out there, the fresh snow was unmarked, but the swing was moving gently to and fro, slowing, as if someone had jumped from it a minute before.

That was a strange Christmas Eve. I did not believe in the supernatural and racked my brain until I provided some explanations. I was lonely, disorientated, tired, my solitude was oppressive and my spirits low. I was awake yet still half dreaming. I longed desperately for Mary's calm, smiling presence beside me but at that moment, I would have welcomed any human company in this silent, empty place.

Before I slept that night, I heard the church bells ring in Christmas but when I woke, in a strange snow-light, I heard scratching sounds again, and then the pattering footsteps, but this time those were on the stairs. I wondered if I had a fever, though I did not feel ill, just confused and troubled. I should get the next day over before going home, where at least there was life in the world outside my windows.

I felt better in the bright morning sunlight that gleamed and danced on the frozen snow, cooked myself a good breakfast and then decided to delve deeper into the house, most of whose rooms I had not even entered.

There were no cellars and having found nothing of interest elsewhere, I made my way to the attic. It ran along the whole house and was disappointingly empty, though goodness knows what I expected to find anyway, when, as I was leaving, I noticed a low door at the end.

The small annexe was crammed with furniture – school desks, chairs, benches, small iron beds, piled on top of one another, old curtains, none of which could have been moved for decades, but then I noticed that some of the chair legs had clumps of wet grass sticking to them, and there was a notable absence of dust. I peered down into the snowy garden. It was completely empty and there was no swing on the lilac tree branch. I had to bend my head under a low beam, and I saw that it had lettering scratched on it.

Jonah. Sara. Sarah. Willm. John. Ellen. Mary. Thom. Silas. Lily. Beth. Dora. Arthur. Thirza. Dorcas. Richard... one or two names were too faded to read. Whose were they? When had they lived here?

I lay awake that night waiting for the sounds of scratching and pattering, I looked out to see if the swing was there again. Nothing. There was a silence so dense that I cried out loud, just to hear the sound of a voice. I was lonelier and more desolate than ever, I longed and then prayed, for the presence of just one other human being in the emptiness of the house and of my own heart.

The clock chimed one, two. At three, the door creaked slightly, opened, though there was no draught. A tapping sounded from below and on descending the stairs, I heard scratching then more tapping, and soft whispers like rustling leaves, becoming more insistent.

I flung open the front door. The sky was clear and frosty, the snow silver white.

I saw nothing but I knew they were there, and when they slipped inside, I felt them brush close to me, as they went pattering across the hall. The door to the snug was ajar though I was certain I had closed it firmly when I went upstairs. I followed them into the room and saw that the fire had not quite died down, but still glowed red at its heart.

They were there, the children, murmuring, sighing softly, making the fire flare again, and gradually they fell still, and as I curled in the armchair, they settled round me, I sensed them, felt them. I was sure that they felt safe. I slept.

I knew that I could never leave here, I was trapped because although I did not know or understand them, I needed these children, as they surely needed me. They had whispered and tapped and ghosted their way in, taken over my hearth as they would surely soon inhabit the rest of the house with me. I must make plans to look after them for the rest of my life, in that Quiet House, where for now at least, the fire blazed, the snow was thick outside, and it was still Christmas.

HUNGER

HUNGER

On the second afternoon, after they had unpacked the last of the boxes, Adrian said they should go out for a walk. That, he said, was the whole point of moving here, to go out for walks.

'Nature,' he said. 'You don't just look at it, do you?'

For the time being she would have been happy to do that. She was bone-tired. Even her brain was tired. Filling the packing cases, cleaning the old flat for the people who were coming in, because that, apparently, was something else you did; travelling down, cleaning the cottage, because the people leaving had not done it for them; unpacking the boxes, putting things away. A hot poker bored into her lower back every time she moved. She had period pain. Her arms ached.

What she wanted to do was indeed to 'just look at it'. To lie down and look at the dense, green leaves that blotted out the mould-coloured sky. The faint line of blue hills in the far distance. The jungle of garden.

'We can get our bearings later,' Adrian said.

Bearings.

She went in search of some painkillers. The bathroom had a sloping roof with a small square of window that let in more greenish, undersea light. The trees pressed in on them, but she supposed that in winter the light would be clear and they would see across fields to the blue hills.

'Paula?'

He bounded up the stairs.

'Come on. What are you doing?'

'Looking for the Nurofen.'

'What's wrong with you?'

She waved a hand vaguely.

'Headache?'

'Back. Arms. You know.'

'You don't need painkillers. You need a walk. Fresh air. Come on.'

She went, not being able to find the Nurofen. Maybe they were in her handbag. Maybe they were slipped in with the bed linen. Or the DVDs.

'Come on!'

The wooden gate felt greasy after the night's rain and the long grass trailed cold against her legs.

Adrian stood in the middle of the track and slowly stretched his arms above his head. Closed his eyes.

Took a deep breath, expanding his rib cage. Released it slowly.

You look so stupid, she wanted to say. But just walked on past him.

'AAAHHHH!' he went again.

The cottage was at the end of the track that opened into a wider lane. There was no other house until you reached a small green at the top.

'Do you think we'll be snowed in?'

Adrian leaped and jumped until he reached her. His mouth was half-open, the huge white teeth grinning.

'Hope so.'

'What?'

He put his arm round her shoulders and pulled her in to him for a second.

'Well, it would be fun and it's all part of living in the country.'

'It snows in the town.'

'Different.'

'How?'

'Oh, you know – town snow melts to slush. It looks dirty.'

'Doesn't country snow?'

'Not in the same way.'

Paula thought it probably did, but said nothing.

He pulled her along.

Past the houses, another lane led steeply downhill. *Unsuitable for Motors.*

It narrowed. Trees on either side, and more trees below. The air mushroomy.

Adrian turned to face her. His forehead was damp.

'You're going to love it. You could come down here every day.'

She tried to imagine that.

'Before you start work.'

'I start work at half past eight.'

'But I'll be gone by seven, and people get up early in the country.'

'What people?'

'Oh, everybody.'

But she liked it. Liked the great smooth tree trunks and the closeness of the air. She looked up. The sky seemed far away.

They dropped down the steep slope, clutching onto one another and suddenly Paula had a leap of the heart, as if this were some sort of mad, secret impulse, rather than a long-planned and several times almost-capsized move from suburban street to isolated village. But it had not capsized. The cottage had not been bought by someone else. They had packed up their lives and despatched them two hundred miles in a van, which had had to make three stabs at reversing down the track to their gate.

They were here, then. She slithered a couple of yards to the point where the hard surface turned to mud.

'What's that?'

Adrian stood sideways, head cocked.

'Sounds like singing.'

'Not singing.'

It was quiet again, apart from the occasional shushing of the leaves.

'There.'

'Sounds like chanting.'

Paula hesitated.

'What?'

'Maybe we shouldn't...disturb them.'

'Disturb who?'

He went crashing on through the undergrowth. The noise stopped.

Eventually, she followed him.

There was a clearing. The ground was level, covered in leaf mould and twigs. Paula smelled burning wood.

They were a few yards away: four children, nine or ten years old. Two girls, two boys. They were crouching or kneeling, and bending forwards to look into something from which a thin spiral of smoke was coiling.

'What are they doing?' She did not know why she whispered.

'Whatever it is they shouldn't be lighting fires in a wood,' Adrian said. But he was whispering, too.

'What have they got?'

They went forward a pace.

The children had started to half-sing, half-chant softly again. They had an old enamel bowl and a stick each; the bowl was balanced on a nest of twigs, which was alight and smoking feebly. Each child took a turn at stirring whatever was in the bowl, while the others watched; then another took over, on and on, stir and stir.

Paula smiled.

'Damn silly,' Adrian said.

'It's hardly alight. The sticks will be quite damp. They're OK.'

Eventually, two of the children lifted the bowl and the oldest child banged on the sticks to extinguish the smouldering. They had a bucket and they poured a greenish liquid into it from the bowl. The two smaller children had lost interest and wandered away.

'Great,' Adrian turned to her, eyes bright. 'Isn't it? Great.'

'But you said – '

'No, no. It wasn't dangerous. There was hardly a spark. No, I meant it's great for kids, playing out in the wild like this, making up their own games.'

'Boy Scouts?'

'No, not Boy Scouts. Boy Scouts are organised – by adults. This is all the kids themselves. I think it's great. It's what they should be doing. It's why we've come here, Paula.'

'We're not kids.'

But she could see he was impatient.

The children had trailed away, two trying to carry the bucket between them.

Adrian stretched, arms high, fingertips splayed out.

'Don't you think that's what they ought to be doing? No dangerous roads, no mindless computer games, out in the fresh air.'

'I was wondering why they aren't at school.'

Adrian was keen on proper schooling.

'When we have our own…'

But they did not have their own.

'It'll be some holiday or other. Country holidays, you know. May Days and so forth.'

'It's the end of June.'

He turned. 'Why do you always have to pick me up when I say anything? Why do you have to pour cold water? You agreed we should move to the country. You wanted to move here.'

Which was true.

They hauled themselves back up the muddy path.

She needed to think about it. Yes, she had agreed. Was that the same as wanting to? She wasn't sure. She agreed to a lot of things.

She thought of lying in bed, looking at the green leaves. Grey sky. Listening to the silence.

'You're not the one having to get a train at seven every morning, commute for over an hour, walk at both ends, rain or shine, leave in the dark, get home in the dark.'

'Well, in winter.'

'You're not the one.'

Was she the one who had wanted to move to the country? After a time they both had, but she couldn't remember where it had begun.

'You are not the one left alone here in a cottage at the end of a lane in a hamlet without anything, without a shop, a pub, a school, a bus, a...'

Not that she needed the pub, school or bus.

Knowing nobody.

'You've always said you prefer your own company.'

Had she?

'Those kids,' he said, taking her hand and swinging it as they went back past the row of cottages.

'I mean, it's a paradise, isn't it? Running loose, perfectly safe.'

'How do you know they're perfectly safe?'

He swung her hand up and kissed it. Smack. His lips were damp.

'You're not worried about the mad axeman?'

'No. I just wonder how you know it's perfectly safe. I mean, why the country would be safer than the town. The city.'

Adrian gave his hyena laugh.

'Traffic. Road rage. Paedophiles. Knife crime. Oh yes, indeed, urban life is very safe.'

'I didn't – '

'Ha! Ha! Ha!'

The Nurofen had begun to wear off. Someone was dragging her insides down at the front and boring the hot poker into her back. The headache was gone, though.

'What do you think they were doing? Cooking something?'

Stone Soup, she remembered.

'Making witches' potions.' Adrian put on a spooky voice. 'Stirring the cauldron. Eye of newt and all that. I think it's great. Really great. All that space. No one telling you what to do. No Nintendo.'

'I don't think children play Nintendo now, do they? Isn't it something else?'

Adrian slammed the gate.

'There you go,' he said. 'Why do always have to

correct me? Why do you have to be right?'

'I wasn't... '

But he had gone thundering up the uncarpeted stairs and crashing into the bathroom.

He had two more days off, during which they sorted out the furniture, the curtains, the kitchen, the linen, the lamps, the books, and Paula forgot what it was like not to ache, not to feel so tired she longed to lie on the floor and sleep without undressing. It rained. Adrian sang and whistled. The electricity failed. The oil delivery came. And every morning and afternoon he made her go out for a walk, to explore, even in the rain, because, he went on saying, that was why they had come here.

'Fresh air. The natural world. Space. Exercise.'

And she had agreed. When they had still been living in Salisbury Road she had agreed, had longed for all of this, the greenness, the space, the silence. She did not blame him at all.

When he went back to work, she would start organising her workroom, an old lean-to conservatory at the back, with a couple of broken panes and rotting wood in the door. But hers. It had a floor of old, uneven bricks and a tortoise stove. She could see the shadows of the blue hills and the sky was soft with cloud, right above her head.

On the second morning she went for a walk alone, ambling along the track and across the field without any sense of direction or purpose. Adrian always had a purpose – to the east, to the west, to the woods, to the fields, to see a view, to reach the end of somewhere. Not having one made her feel peaceful.

On the far side of the field, beside a high hedge, she could see them again: a little cluster of children close together, arms stretched up, then backs bent, arms up and bent. Paula zigzagged quietly towards them.

They were picking unripe berries, green and small, and dropping them into a plastic tub.

'You do know you can't eat those?'

Two of the children turned and stared at her, but did not smile or speak.

'Leave them till autumn. They're OK when they're ripe.'

One of the boys stripped a handful of the green berries and ate them, looking her straight in the eye.

'You'll get tummy ache.'

But after a moment, during which they merely stared at her in silence and unsmiling, she turned away.

'Wonderful,' Adrian would have said, 'foraging for their own treats, not buying all that sugary junk from a shop. That's how it should be.'

Paula wondered again why they were not in school.

She began to notice the birds that came into the garden. While she was at her drawing board or painting at her table she kept looking up and spotting a blackbird under the bushes, a thrush on the fence, a long-tailed tit, a great tit, chaffinches. Once or twice a woodpecker swooped in, flashing scarlet and white. They did not fly up in panic. She put breadcrumbs on the step and they were gone within the hour.

At the weekend they drove to the nearest market town for groceries and she bought a bag of bird nuts and a plastic feeder. An extra loaf.

'How is it,' she asked Adrian, 'on the train?'

'Well, it's a train. I go on it.'

'I mean...how are you finding it? The commute? Do you enjoy it?'

'Does anyone?'

He went to bed just after nine-thirty and was often curt with her. But when they went out for a walk in the sunshine on Saturday he said, 'This is what it's all about, you know. This is it.'

'What?'

'Life,' he said, raising his voice slightly. 'This is what life is all about.'

And gradually Paula found that it was. The first surprise was how much she loved being alone for twelve hours a day; how much she resented the people pressing in on her when she went to the supermarket or into town. She moved slightly away to avoid being touched, sat in the café drinking her coffee alone, watching them and feeling as if she belonged to some other species than theirs. She did not feel hostile, just detached. Different. She lived in an invisible shell.

The cottage was quiet, apart from wind in the leaves. Rain on the leaves. Rain on the glass roof of the lean-to. A distant tractor in the fields. The postman's van. Birdsong.

The days slid into one another and in the afternoons she sometimes felt a mist of tiredness settle on her like a cobweb, and she would sleep, on the couch or the bed, or, now that the days were warmer, on the grass. She woke gently, to lie still, not thinking, listening, watching the shadow of the leaves moving across the bedroom ceiling or the sun's brightness on a sheet of white paper.

It was on one of the fine, warm afternoons, when she had been sleeping on the grass, that she woke more suddenly than usual, because of a different sound: a shuffle and then a half-stifled murmur. She opened her eyes and saw the children. There were only two of them this time, the tallest and the smallest. The girl was standing under the hanging bird feeder, extracting peanuts one by one and handing them down to the small boy, who put them quickly into his pocket. In between hiding them, both children were eating nuts as well. Occasionally, the girl glanced round quickly, but her hands were deft and swift and as Paula watched the nuts in the feeder went down, until it was empty.

She was going to jump up and challenge them, partly annoyed about the theft, but also with concern. Weren't peanuts meant for birds, 'unfit for human consumption'? But almost as the thought came into her mind the children were gone, vanishing like shadows when the sun goes in, soft and swift of foot, down the path and out not through the gate but through a neat gap they had made in the hedge. The shrubby branches closed behind them and the garden was empty.

The next thought in her mind seemed urgent. She would not tell Adrian. Must not tell Adrian. Why was that so important?

She got up and re-filled the nut feeder and for the rest of the day was alert for the slightest sound or sight of the children. But they did not come back.

Not that day. Not the next, and then it was the weekend and they went for more energetic walks and still she did not tell him. When they were not walking or grocery shopping, Adrian slept. Paula had started to tackle the jungle that was the garden, slashing back, raking out, digging up, while he slept on. She did not mind. She liked her own company after all.

The fine weather settled in.

'My mother wants to come,' Adrian said.

'She wouldn't like it here. Yvonne likes the town. Shops. Stuff like that.'

'*Stuff like that.*'

'I just meant – what would she do all day? I've only done half these illustrations. I can't leave it.'

'She'll come on Tuesday. You can go out with her in the afternoons, can't you? You don't work all day, do you?'

'Well...most of it.'

She had not told him about the sleeping.

'There you are, then. And take her for some walks. Do you both good.'

'Be part of the natural world.'

'Exactly! You see?'

His face was an open beam of satisfaction. He had taught her something. He liked to teach people.

'Tuesday, but she wouldn't get here till lunchtime. Give you a morning for work, won't it?'

She was not taking Yvonne to the supermarket. 'You need this. You don't tell me you manage without that?

You don't tell me you have never bought...?...No, Paula, you shouldn't ever buy *that* brand, they force-feed Third World babies with bottle milk...Put it back, pure waste of money, the own-brand is fine...But Adrian doesn't like sausages...'

She went alone on the Monday morning. It was quiet. A few mothers with babies perched in the trolleys wheeled slowly round in pairs, chatting. Paula shopped without a list, without a system, enjoying the wander from aisle to aisle, looking at books and make-up she would never buy, before homing in on all her usual stuff. She had coffee, filled up with petrol, bought a newspaper and chocolate from the kiosk. Sang on the way home.

Yvonne would be here tomorrow, but she had done the shopping without her.

Slowly the cottage had stopped being the cottage and become home. Things had found permanent resting places, the smell of mice had faded, the curtains hung straight. Adrian fell asleep during television programmes. She had begun to tame the garden. But whereas a house stayed as you left it, a garden ran away with you and after a week of hands burning from nettles and thumbs scratched with thorns, Paula lost heart and just mowed enough grass to sleep on. The rest ran riot.

'That's a mess,' Adrian said. 'When are you going to start on it?'

'It's nature.'

He turned away.

Five minutes later he was in bed, asleep.

There was a full moon. She sat out on the grass, looking at the pale, ghostly light on some white phlox which had appeared by the hedge. There was a night scene in the children's book she was illustrating. She looked carefully at the white petals. Her bloodless white hand. The silver stones on the wall. Something barked. Something rustled low down among the bushes.

She felt happy.

'I heard something,' Yvonne said. She wore a black satin dressing gown with a scarlet dragon in raised embroidery on the back.

'It's always quiet here at night. Did you sleep well?'

'Bit too quiet. You get used to traffic noise; I suppose it lulls you to sleep. But whatever it was woke me up and it was barely six o'clock.'

'Adrian is up at twenty past.'

'It wasn't Adrian.'

'What sort of noise?'

'I wouldn't have said it was a noise. A sound. More a sound.'

Paula set the coffee pot down on the kitchen table.

'But you slept all right on the whole?'

Yvonne reached for the sugar. Her fingernails were painted navy blue, but the edges were chipped. Paula thought that if you wore nail varnish in startling colours you had to maintain them.

'Adrian looks very washed out.'

'It's a long commute.'

'Up so early, home so late. I don't understand it.'

'He loves being in the country.'

Yvonne gave her an unpleasant look.

'We'll go for a walk later. I have to finish something off that I left to dry last night.'

'Oh don't pay any attention to me. I can amuse myself.'

'No, but we will. Go for a walk I mean.'

Paula noticed at once, as soon as she walked into the workroom. The drawing board had been moved, only slightly, but she would have noticed even a centimetre. And the side window was slightly ajar.

It was not until later that she noticed that the chocolate had gone. She had eaten two squares and folded the paper over the open end of the bar. It had been on the table, to the right of her pencil pot.

Yvonne wandered in.

'Oh heavens, sorry, sorry. I always forget that you don't.'

She dropped the cigarette on the brick floor, crushed it to and fro under her heel and left it there.

Paula said nothing. Adrian would, when he came home and smelled smoke in the house. She would leave it to Adrian. She was his mother.

'Shall we go out, then?'

Yvonne lit a fresh cigarette the moment the front door closed behind them. Paula said nothing, only picked up the spent match from the path where her mother-in-law had thrown it.

'We generally go this way – past the houses and down into the wood. Well, not much of a wood but, you know…I love trees.'

It was warm, slightly damp. Misty.

'I'd go mad,' Yvonne said. 'Never seeing anybody.'

'I like it. I like my own company.'

Yvonne looked at her sideways.

'What do you do at the weekends, when Adrian's home?'

'Go for walks. You know.'

'What will it be like for him in winter? Out of the

house in the dark, home in the dark. Not much fun, you know.'

'Moving here was his idea,' Paula said.

Yvonne grabbed her arm as the track sloped down between the trees.

'Where does this lead?'

'We come out at the bottom into a clearing, then cross the field.'

'With animals?'

'With…'

Rabbits, badgers, foxes flitted through her mind.

'Cows? Bulls?'

'Oh no. It's perfectly safe'

Yvonne stopped to light another cigarette.

'I'm not much of a one for fields. Shall we go back?'

She walked quite smartly once they were on the level again, so that she reached the cottage gate first, just as all four of the children were sneaking round from the back. The eldest, in front, had her hands full of something; the boy behind was cramming a handful of cornflakes into his mouth from the open box he carried. The small ones came up behind. One held a packet of biscuits.

'Oh my God!'

Paula pushed past Yvonne and put out her arm to catch hold of the girl at the front.

'It was you,' she said, without any anger. 'You came and took the chocolate.'

The eyes were wary and also defiant.

'Who on earth are these children? Do you know them, Paula? Where are they from? What are they doing coming out of your house? Why aren't they in school? Have you been stealing? Why aren't you at school?' Yvonne spoke loudly, as if the children were deaf. 'I'm going to call the police.'

'No.'

'They've been in your house. They've been stealing, it's perfectly clear. Don't just let it go, Paula. You turn a blind eye and they'll be back.'

'Will you please leave me to deal with this, Yvonne? Go into the house.'

The children were now pressed together as a single unit, like small animals. Their hair was matted, their faces dirty.

'What were you doing?' Paula said. 'You took the chocolate, you ate the peanuts from the bird feeder, now you've been in and…' she gestured at the food. 'Where do you come from?'

They were mute, staring and still.

'You shouldn't just walk into people's houses. You know that, don't you?'

The small boy clutched the biscuits to his chest.

'Those will break,' Paula said. 'If you hug them.'

The mist had thickened to a drizzle, muffling the air.

No word was spoken and she did not see any signal pass between them. One minute they were standing together in their hostile silence, the next they were running, down the path and through the open gate, making almost no sound, flashing away like birds between the high hedges. A few cornflakes drifted down in their wake and settled on the ground.

'They'll be back, you know.' Yvonne said. 'You should call the police.'

'Oh, I don't think so. Would you like some coffee?'

'Is it real or instant?'

'I don't buy instant. The police are miles away...'

'It's that sort of inertia they rely on. Nobody being bothered to report them.'

'Yvonne, they're children – young children. The last thing they need is the police involved in their lives from the very start.'

The glass of the cafetiere cracked as she banged it down. Yvonne firmed her lips together.

Adrian did not get home until after nine that night. The train line was unreliable; they had been held up by another signalling failure. There were bruise-coloured smears beneath his eyes.

'Signalling failure. Engine failure. Driver failure – failure to turn up.'

He fell onto the sofa so hard the springs bounced.

'We had a burglary,' Yvonne said.

Adrian sat up.

Paula wanted to slap her. 'Well, hardly.'

'What else do you call it? They were stealing. They came into this house while we were out and stole things. I call that a burglary.'

'They only took food.'

'Oh, so taking food isn't burglary?'

'They're children. They are less than ten years old.'

'A child can be held morally responsible from the age of seven.'

Her voice was oily with satisfaction.

'You mean you caught them at it?'

'Only I wasn't allowed to phone the police.'

Adrian lay back again and closed his eyes.

'Paula?' He sounded infinitely weary.

'They're children. You saw them in the wood that day. You know the ones. You said it was wonderful.'

'What was wonderful?'

'That they could be roaming about freely, enjoying nature.'

'Roaming about freely thieving from other people,' Yvonne said. 'Where do they live, these children? You'll need to tell their parents.'

'We'll see.'

Paula took the empty mugs into the kitchen, dumped them in the sink and went outside. It had rained again. The air smelled of wet leaves, wet grass, damp earth. A blackbird sang.

She went to the bottom of the garden and stood very still, wondering what she ought to do about the children. Not the police, of course, and she had no idea where they came from. She could follow them, the next time, but they appeared and disappeared like wraiths.

She had no thought of accosting their parents, but she wanted to know what their home was like and why they did what they did. Why they were not at school.

A light went on in the front bedroom, but she knew Yvonne would still be downstairs, waiting. When she had married Adrian her sister Elaine had said, 'You do know it's normal for mothers of only sons to hate the women they marry, don't you? She'll give you grief.'

Elaine's own marriage had lasted barely two years, but as Ted's mother was dead before they met, Paula had not understood how Elaine knew all the things about which she preached with such apparent authority. She had not thought a great deal about Yvonne in advance, but then she sometimes thought that she had not thought a great deal about Adrian, either. He had pursued her – wooed her, Elaine said sarcastically – with such ferocity and determination, such eagerness and puppy-like ardour that she had been unable to put up any resistance, unable to see him clearly, unable to imagine what their future might be like. It had been easy to let herself be swept along. She was by nature quite lazy and a sort of inertia had stifled her, blurring her usually sharp critical sense. She had been very fond of Adrian. Who could not be? He hadn't a bone of malice in his body, never complained, always enthused, was optimistic to a fault, all of which was refreshing to someone who was inclined to occasional melancholy. Yvonne had existed, vaguely, but lived miles away from them. That her doing so meant she would come to stay for a week or more at a time was another thing Paula had not bargained for.

Over the past nine years she had learned how to deal with Yvonne's visits simply by carrying on as usual and letting Yvonne follow or not, accompany her or stay at home. It had worked quite well. Sometimes Yvonne came with her – to the art supplier, the shops, the park or a garden centre, to have coffee or even lunch out. Sometimes she did not, but put her feet up on the sofa and read crime novels. And waited – counting the minutes, Paula always thought – until Adrian returned from work.

They did not much like one another, she and Yvonne, but nor did they argue. There was no feeling between them energetic enough to spark off rows.

Yvonne was sitting in the half-dark, book on her lap.

'Adrian is worn out.'

'He soon makes up his sleep at the weekend.'

'It's this commuting.'

Paula did not answer. Her mother-in-law was right, of course, but it was not something she felt like discussing when his travelling was inevitable, a fact of their lives. It wasn't as if he had not thought about it all before they had moved.

'Don't you ever ask yourself if you're being selfish?'

Paula was startled.

'It's all very well for you down here, everything cosy, just enjoying the countryside and doing your painting.'

'I work,' Paula said. 'What you call "your painting" is work. I get paid for it. We couldn't manage without.'

'Are you telling me Adrian isn't the breadwinner around here?'

'We both are. I'll lock up now, Yvonne. You only need to switch the lights off when you come up.'

'And what about children?'

'I've already told you, I am not calling the police. I'll try and find out a bit more about them and, of course, I'll speak to them if they come here again, don't worry – I don't approve of letting them get away with theft any more than you do. But they're very young. It isn't a police matter. Not at the moment anyway.'

'I did not,' Yvonne said, 'mean those children.'

Paula had never said that she did not like children, that children made her uneasy. She was nervous of them. She did not like the way they stared without smiling, felt judged by the stares. Judged, she thought now, slipping out of her jeans and T-shirt in the dark bedroom, by the stares of the children who had broken into the cottage and eaten the bird nuts, the four unsmiling, silent children.

Yvonne had raised the subject only two or three times in all their nine years and apparently never expected an answer to what had not exactly been a question. Why had they no children, she and Adrian? Because Paula did not like them and Adrian did not care enough to insist. If she had become pregnant, he would have taken to being a father as eagerly as he took to everything, regressing even more deeply into childhood himself as a result. But as she had not, he sailed along cheerfully with her alone.

She lay beside him on her back now, hands behind

her head. She always left the curtains open. There was a
moon, gliding majestically up the sky. Adrian breathed
quietly. He was a quiet sleeper.

Images of the children were in her mind, stuffing
their mouths with sour berries and bird nuts, sneaking
out of her house with the biscuits and the box of cereal.
Always, they looked straight at her, unsmiling, solemn,
hostile, defiant.

She sat up. Little thieves. They were little Gypsies,
ragged, running-wild thieves, the rural equivalent of
streetwise.

The next time it would be tins and packets and jars,
and then they would move on to the ornaments: silver
box and knives, her paints, the laptop, Adrian's coin
collection. They thieved to order, surely. No group of
such young children would think it up for themselves.
The stirring game, the hedgerow berries, that was one
thing. None of that mattered, even though they should
clearly have been in school. And it was none of her
business. But coming into the cottage and stealing was
something else and they had been told to do it by adults.

She went to sleep abruptly, her thoughts snapped off
midway and the children's unsmiling faces shifted about
in her mind, now shadowy, now clear, all night, all night.

The sun shone. She had almost finished her illustrations.

'What are you going to do about it?'

Adrian rubbed his hair with the flat of his hand. It was Saturday.

'About what?'

He dipped his forefinger into the butter and rolled it round, then into the sugar bowl, then sucked his finger.

'That is disgusting.'

He shrugged.

'You're not really going to ring the police are you?'

'Of course I'm not.'

'Good. They're just…'

Paula moved the butter. 'Enjoying the natural world around them?'

'Thing is, they have the sort of freedom without boundaries that town kids never dream of.'

'Town kids nick things.'

'Come on…a few cornflakes?'

Yvonne walked through the kitchen in her dressing gown on her way to light a cigarette outside.

Adrian made a gesture behind her back for 'When is she going?'

The day Yvonne went they lay in the sun all afternoon with bottles of beer and bags of crisps and apples, and dozed and read and Adrian said he had never felt so light of heart. He used the actual words. Light of heart.

'But you hate the commute.'

'No, no, I'm used to it and it's worth it, isn't it? Worth it for all this.'

He made a vague sweep of his arm.

'The green. Trees. Fresh air.'

'Nature's bounty.'

He glanced at her, but Paula's face was solemn.

'Well yes. You like it, don't you? I mean, you're happy? You wouldn't want to go back? Back there?' He seemed to need reassurance.

'No. I wouldn't want to go back. There.'

'So you're happy?'

'Of course I am,' Paula said.

She could not have begun to explain just how happy. She did not think she had admitted it to herself. Happy here. Happy every day she woke. Happy alone. Happy to see no one at all from the time she barely stirred when Adrian's alarm went to the moment she heard him open the gate in the evening. Happy to lie on a rug in the garden or on her bed, looking at the trees. Working peacefully. Making tea. Clearing a bit more of the garden. Alone. Happy. She had met no one since they had arrived here except the postman and a woman walking a black dog. Unless you counted the children.

She could not have told him that she dreaded the weekends, when he was at home, not because she no longer loved him – she loved him as much as she ever had, which was probably not a great deal. She liked to be alone here, that was all.

The summer grew hotter. Paula could work only early in the morning because the lean-to became stifling. She read undemanding books and then just looked up at the leaves that hung heavy and still.

Adrian – jovial on Friday night, because he had a week's holiday coming – suggested they go to the nearest village for a pub supper, which they ate at a table in the garden: home-cooked ham, eggs, chips, peas. Real ale.

'None of this gourmet-dining rubbish,' he said, wiping bread round the last smears of yolk. 'Ruin of good pubs, that's been. Coulis of this and scented with that.'

She agreed. Agreeing was a relief. They held hands, walking back through the still, July night, stomachs bloated.

'Best move we ever made.' Adrian belched softly. She agreed again.

He sat in a deckchair most of the week, reading American crime novels recommended by Yvonne, while Paula worked. She looked up occasionally and saw him, legs splayed below khaki shorts, and felt irritable, her precious, solitary days invaded, time stolen.

'Who needs to go away on holiday?' Adrian said more than once.

She sent him out for walks, pleading work as an excuse for not joining him, and he strode off, looking conscientiously around.

'So much to see, if only you lift your eyes. People just don't look.'

He waved an arm.

The second time she was left alone, she came out of the lean-to when she was sure he was away up the lane and first heard something rustle, then the scrape of the gate. She waited in the doorway and saw a small shadow.

'Hello?'

The girl froze.

'Where are you going?'

No reply, only the stare.

'You're going to have to talk to me about this, you know. About coming here and trying to sneak in and take things. Where are the others?'

When Paula went nearer to the girl, she saw something in her eyes as well as defiance, some wariness, and felt the tension in the thin body, poised, ready to streak away again.

'There's a jug of lemonade. Do you want some?'

She went past the girl without touching her and into

the kitchen, took the lemonade from the fridge, two glasses. A shadow fell across the doorway.

'You can come in.'

A couple of steps, but no more. Paula set the drinks on the table, with a packet of biscuits.

The child had dark brown hair in matted ringlets, a boys' checked shirt and shorts. Her eyes were thickly lashed.

Paula drank her own lemonade.

'I'm Paula.'

The girl dived forwards and grabbed three biscuits deftly off the plate.

'Don't eat like that, you'll choke. Wash them down with this.'

But she gobbled the biscuits, then drank. Her face puckered up.

'Sorry. It is a bit sharp.'

'S'not lemonade.'

'Yes it is. I made it. With lemons. There's some milk.'

She got a carton from the fridge. When she turned round, the child was pushing three more biscuits into her mouth and the last one into the pocket of her shorts.

'I could make you some toast.'

Paula watched the milk drain down the glass, as in a speeded-up film.

She made three rounds of toast with butter and strawberry jam.

Starving children happened in Africa, not here in rural England, she thought as the child ate, this land of plenty and supermarkets twenty minutes away. Shame flooded through her. She had not realised until now that the leaf soup and unripe berries, the bird nuts, were free food for empty bellies. She made two more slices of toast, but as she started to butter them Adrian came in through the door, red-faced and perspiring, his shirt tied round his waist. His pale upper body was damp.

'What on earth's going on?'

The child was trying to bolt, clutching the toast, but could not get out, because Adrian's thick body was blocking the doorway.

'It's OK,' she said, 'sit down again. It's only Adrian. He doesn't mind.'

'Who the hell said I didn't mind?' He threw his shirt onto the floor. 'Are we feeding the neighbourhood kids now or what?'

The girl's eyes were wide with alarm. Paula reached out and tried to lead her back to the table, but she pulled away, wire-taut at the touch.

'I don't even know your name.'

'She's in here stuffing herself with our food and she hasn't even told you who she is?'

'Shut up!'

He looked astonished and in his astonishment, stepped forwards.

The girl was out of the door and away, her feet soundless on the path.

'For God's sake, Paula.'

'No, actually, for God's sake, Adrian. Why did you frighten her like that? That child's hungry – heaven knows when she last ate a proper meal.'

'And it's all down to us to remedy that, is it? You know what'll happen, don't you? Come six o'clock the lot of them will be round here and you'll be giving them a full cooked meal, and where do you suppose it will end? Next thing, they'll be living here.'

'No,' Paula said, clearing the crockery. 'They won't. But if they come back for more food, they can have it. Have you ever been hungry?'

'Well of course I've been hungry. So have you – everyone's been hungry.'

'Yes and known where the next meal was coming from and when. Not the same.'

He stood at the sink, sloshing cold water over his face and shoulders. The water sprayed over the draining board onto the floor.

'You could have a cold shower,' Paula said.

For the week that he was home there was no sign of

the children. Adrian insisted on their taking numerous walks, in spite of the heat.

'Gypsies,' he said one day, panting up the slope between overhanging trees. 'They'll have moved on. You could tell they were Gypsy kids.'

'How?'

'Thieving. Never at school. Besides, they had a Gypsy look.'

'A Gypsy look?'

'You know what I mean. Swarthy.'

'The little boys were quite fair.'

Adrian pushed ahead of her as the path widened.

On Monday he left at seven o'clock for work and by nine two of the children were hanging about near the gate.

'If those kids come back, you don't feed them, OK? It's like stray cats. Once you start...'

She made a pile of toast and took it out to them, with a bought fruitcake. They snatched and ran. Paula followed.

It was a caravan, parked in the corner of a field, hidden behind a thicket away from the road and the houses. She saw them streak along, keeping close to the hedge, and disappear inside. Through the open door she saw a table and a woman's back against the light. After a few moments the woman came out. There was a white plastic garden chair beside the caravan steps in which she sat heavily and turned her face to the sun.

Everything went quiet. Paula went on, keeping so close to the hedge that brambles scraped her bare arms.

The caravan was quite large with a gas cylinder attached to the back and a rainwater butt. Two of the children, the boys, had come to the doorway and were staring at Paula in the usual hostile way, eyes like pebbles.

The girl appeared behind them.

'Ma.'

It was almost a whisper, like a warning.

The woman opened her eyes.

'Sorry,' Paula said. 'Sorry. I didn't mean to startle you.'

'What the fuck do you think you're doing?'

The children huddled together.

'Creeping up like that. Who the fuck are you?' She half-turned her head. 'You lot get back in.'

The huddle vanished.

'Oh, I get it. You're the one that hands out food. What the fuck do you mean by that?'

Paula cleared her throat.

'We don't need handouts. We're not charity cases.'

'I was only – they seemed hungry.'

'Yes, well they're not.'

'They ate what I gave them.'

''Course they did, they're kids – what do you expect?'

'They were eating the bird nuts.'

The woman laughed. It was hard to tell her age.

'And berries.'

'How long you lived round here? They'll eat anything. Why not?'

'The berries weren't ripe and the bird nuts – they're not really for humans to eat.'

The woman laughed again and hauled herself out of the chair.

'Just leave them be.'

'Shouldn't your children be at school?'

But she was climbing the steps back into the caravan.

'You sod off,' she said without looking round.

Paula glimpsed the children behind her. The van was in full sun and she imagined them inside the hot space, crowded together, fractious, tempers short. She wondered if they were beaten. The thought was upsetting, but there was nothing she could do. Eventually she had to retreat.

'What did I tell you?'

The heat was making Adrian bad tempered at the end of every day.

'You've brought it on yourself. Of course they're not hungry. They get every benefit going. They're taking you for a mug.'

He went out into the humid garden with a can of beer.

If they were not hungry would they be bothered to steal food? She looked at her painting of a badger disappearing down a hole.

Why would they?

They had wolfed down the toast as if they hadn't eaten for days. Was that what children normally did? She doubted it.

Adrian had taken off his shirt and shoes, and was lying on the grass with the beer can held to his chest.

'Like a cattle truck,' he said, 'going and coming back. Worse coming back. You don't know what heat's like until you've been on that six thirty train.'

They were not eating till late on these nights and Adrian went up to bed immediately afterwards. The food lay heavy on his stomach, making him snore. Paula had taken to sleeping on a rug in the garden. Only a brief dawn chill and the dew sent her inside, an hour before his alarm went off.

She lay thinking of the girl, cramming hot toast into her mouth.

No one would eat like that if they weren't ravenous. No child would munch bird nuts and steal half-boxes of cornflakes.

The alarm sounded.

Adrian groaned and pushed back the single sheet.

Paula woke to the sound of his raised voice coming from outside.

'I'll take my belt to you, do you hear me? And I'm sending for the police. We're sick of you. Now bugger off!'

Paula raced downstairs.

'Little sods. Opened the door and they were in here, in this kitchen. Helping themselves to that.'

The half-eaten custard tart had been under cling film.

'You encouraged them. You started this.'

She did not go out shopping until late afternoon, when the sky had turned inky and the air was so moist she felt as if she were trying to breathe underwater. The storm broke as she was checking out, crashing directly overhead. She went to the café and sat watching the car park flood and felt as if she were waiting for something, suspended between two places, two worlds.

'It's unreal,' a woman at the next table said.

Adrian sent a text to say his train was delayed: 'f...ing line flooded'. She had another coffee.

When she got back, the lane was awash with earth and branches and stones. The front path was a stream.

But it was not the storm that had broken open the door and smashed a couple of panes in the lean-to; not the storm that had smeared her paints all over her half-finished work; not the storm that had thrown china onto the kitchen floor, deposited excrement on the worktop and left puddles of urine on the floor.

Paula sat down, shaking.

Thunder grumbled in the distance and the sky was sulphurous.

When Adrian got in just after ten she was still sitting there in the half-dark.

'Bugger' he said, standing in the doorway, his hair plastered to his forehead. 'Oh bugger.'

She expected him to blame her, but he did not. He said nothing at all, just dropped his jacket onto the chair and helped her clear up, unloaded the car and put the groceries away, taped a piece of plywood over the broken windows.

He ate some cold ham and tomatoes, with chunks of bread torn off the new loaf. Paula ate nothing.

'It's them, of course,' he said through a mouthful of pink meat. 'You do know it's them? This can't go on.'

'It could have been anyone.'

'But it wasn't.'

Adrian put his plate in the sink.

'You should eat,' he said.

She opened the back door and stood on the step. The

storm had retreated, the air cooled. Water was running down the lane and dripping off the trees. What had it been like in that caravan, parked in an open field? What if the roof leaked, the windows let in water? What if their beds were soaking wet? They had taken what food there had been in the kitchen, but that wasn't much. What if...?

Her brain swirled. The clouds parted to show a clear patch of night sky.

She went inside.

'I think this is it,' Adrian said the next morning. He had called in sick. 'After last night I do feel sick, in actual fact.' He had brought tea and got back into bed. 'I really think this is it.'

'What is what?'

'To begin with, I never realised what the commute would be like. Never imagined it. Which I really should have done. You should look at a thing from all sides.'

Paula sat up. Beyond the window the sky was pearl grey and the air coming through it was fresh.

'And you're lonely.'

She looked round at him. 'I'm not lonely.'

'Of course you are or you wouldn't have had those kids round all the time.'

'I didn't...'

'I don't blame you, Paula. I understand, actually. It's obvious you've been lonely and I should have seen it. I've been a bit selfish.'

Her mouth worked, but no words came out. She did not fully understand him.

'We don't have to go back to Salisbury Road. We could try a bit further in. There's that nice new development at Ashtree.'

'What are you talking about?'

But it was obvious. She looked at him and saw the light of determination in his eyes.

'I'm happy here,' she said. 'I don't want to live on a new development.'

'Of course you're not happy.'

Paula repeated to herself what he had just said. How had she not understood before now? She had simply never realised.

'And the commute is killing me. Oh, the weekends are great, going for our walks, being surrounded by...' He waved his hand.

'Nature.'

'Exactly.'

'But how much of it do I get to see otherwise? It's OK for you.'

'Yes,' Paula said. 'It is.' Because it was and the walks had nothing to do with it.

'I'm sorry it hasn't worked out, but with these kids wrecking the place...We'll have to be careful about that, by the way – not to mention it.'

'I thought you were going to phone the police.'

'Best left, I think. I mean, on reflection. No, I meant not mention it to prospective buyers.'

'There won't be any.'

'Don't be ridiculous. Of course there will. This is a dream cottage. That's why we bought it. Our dream cottage.'

'It's still mine.'

'You'll be much better off at Ashtree. I'll check out the website.'

'No.'

'They're bound to have a website.'

'I mean, no, don't bother to check it out. Unless you want to go to Ashtree on your own. It would probably suit you.'

'You ought to stay in bed today. You had a nasty experience. You're not yourself.'

'I am, actually. That is exactly what I am – myself. I'm staying here by myself. If I have to.'

'You're still in shock.'

'No,' Paula said.

Adrian moved out the following week.

'It isn't permanent, you know,' he said. 'It's only until

you come to your senses.'

He tried to put his arm round her, but she dodged it.

The night after he left she walked round the cottage, then round the garden, then up and down the lane, feeling as if she might take off and float. It was warm again but clear, the moon like a wire. Quiet. She made tea and sat on the grass, trying to remember when Adrian had started to talk about moving to the country, when she had started to take him seriously, when it had become her own want, stronger than his, but for different reasons. He had tried it on to see if it would fit, half-serious, then in panic when he found himself here. She had slipped into it as into the right skin.

The children had not been back. The damage and mess had been a gesture and once made, needn't be repeated. It had almost certainly not been done by them anyway. They had gone home, crying, talking about policemen and the adults had taken matters into their own hands.

But now that Adrian had gone Paula felt she had permission to worry about them again. When she saw them she would say they could come whenever they liked.

She did not see them and after three days she walked up to the field, carrying a bag of crisps and some apples.

If the woman was there, she would try and speak to her and explain. Apologise.

The field was empty. The grass where the caravan had been was pressed down and yellowed and there were muddy grooves, but otherwise no sign that it had been there at all. Paula scuffed the grass back into place here and there with the side of her shoe and for a moment felt as if the space that had contained them and the van in which they lived was still full of them. But it was not.

That night she boiled two eggs and set them on a plate with salad and bread and butter, but when she sat down at the table she felt nauseous and could not eat. In the morning she left her cereal untouched. Her throat constricted when she looked at it.

She drank, tea, coffee, water, ate a few squares of chocolate. Nothing else for days. The cottage was deathly quiet. She walked out sometimes, down the slope between the trees, and saw the ghosts of the children stirring the leaf soup, heard their footsteps on the path as they grabbed the bird nuts and pattered away, their pockets full. It rained, then it was hot again. She stopped working. Her paints dried up in their pots.

Adrian rang.

'It's a great house,' he said. 'Small, but it's detached.

You wouldn't be bothered by the neighbours. It's got a south-facing garden.'

'Trees?'

'Well, they've put some little ones in, attached to those wooden posts, you know. They'll soon grow. Quite a few kids.' He laughed. 'Look properly fed, of course.'

'Ah.'

'How are the little Gypsies?'

'Fine.' Paula said. 'They're fine.'

'They been round again?'

'Oh yes. Certainly. I make them toast and cake. You know.'

'Paula, I warned you.'

'Yes. You did.'

'I think I've been very patient.'

'Yes,' Paula said. 'You have.'

'So when are you moving over here? When are you coming to your senses?'

Paula looked out of the window. It was raining again, a soft veil of rain drifting across the grass.

'Never,' she said. 'No. Probably never.'

It was joyous, dancing in the rain. No one saw her. When she was soaked through she went inside, smiling to herself and made toast. Four slices. Buttered them. Ate them, watching the rain mist the windows of the lean-to. The broken pane was still patched with the plywood Adrian had taped over it.

One day, she would get it properly fixed.

IRISH TWINS

IRISH TWINS

Mary and Fern Piper shared a bedroom in the new place, which their mother called a cottage though it did not look like one. But they had separate windows to look out of and they guarded their individual views fiercely, having nothing else that was not shared, though Mary minded less about this than Fern, because she had the infinite consolation of being the elder by ten months. They were 'Irish twins', born in January and November of the same year. To be Irish twins was not only a blessed thing, their mother told them, but a very rare one and they had always believed it and felt especially marked out.

They moved to the new place when Mary was twelve and Fern still eleven and within the first few days, were shaken to discover that another pair of Irish twins lived in the village, cutting them off at the knees and rendering them altogether less rare and remarkable. But after a while Mary and Fern shrugged and accepted things, finding far more in the new life that was interesting and strange and required both investigation and adjustment. Their mother never quite recovered. Having Irish twins had given her something which set her apart in an otherwise mundane life, something most people crave, after all – to have some mark to distinguish them. Lou Piper knew well enough in her heart that having Irish twins was a small enough claim to significance. Nevertheless, she had made the most of that claim, burnishing and polishing it until it shone, so that when she found out that the Beak brothers were also Irish twins, she felt not only her claim but her whole life to be tarnished. Worse, the Beaks were even closer to one another in age, Jim having been born in early January, Norman in October. The fact that they were four decades older than Mary and Fern was irrelevant. The Beaks had been born and had lived in this village all their lives and naturally they had established precedence.

The place had little in it of charm or attractiveness and was laid out along a minor road with such centre as there was focusing upon the crossroads by the church and the closed public house. The Piper girls did not wonder why they had come to live in it, as the very young do not. They just accepted it and got on with living there, each spending a lot of time looking out from her individual window. Mary's faced the small section of lane and the few houses to the east of the church, Fern's, the row of cottages beside the empty pub. They quickly learned that the Beak brothers lived one on each side, Jim in the middle cottage of a row beside the pub and Norman in a loaf-shaped house just past the church.

The Pipers arrived in July and so had eight weeks free to look out and gradually learn who came and went and why, and discover whatever else happened on each separate side. Very little did. Sometimes, a small herd of cows was moved from the field on the east of the village to another on the west. Two women walked their dogs beneath Mary's window, a man pushed a bicycle, though never seemed to ride it. The dustcart and the post van were seen first by one of the girls and, a second or two later, by the other. A woman with a push-chair stopped under Fern's window to speak to someone who was out of sight. Otherwise, there were the Beak brothers.

It was a dull summer with almost continuous rain falling from clouds that ballooned out of the hills to the west. The Pipers went nowhere, except once, twelve miles on the bus to buy new shoes in town. The cottage was dark and needed whitewashing, which their mother mainly did herself, only helped by their father on his two-week leave. But there were raised voices and soon enough the girls understood that nothing changed or would change, with their move to the new place.

"You're worse than useless. You think you can come here to be waited on. Well, you can think again."

"Go out and walk the five miles to the pub, get out from under this pair of steps."

"We're better off when you're not here."

Every sentence was polished with frequent use.

When the girls came into the room their father smiled weakly, all watery blue eyes and stained teeth and the smell of tobacco. His daughters vied with one another to love him the most but they rarely saw him, barely knew him and they only loved the word and the idea of a father.

To avoid being caught in the line of fire from flying insults they spent hours looking out of their windows, until Fern suggested they should each keep a log of who came and went and at exactly what times.

"...so that we can see a pattern and spot if there is a change."

"Why?"

"It might be useful."

"Who to?"

"I don't know. But spies do it."

And so that summer they became spies, until they grew bored with the lack of incident and the unchanging routine of the milk float and the post van. There was very little of interest to write down in the notebooks.

The only people whose movements they recorded regularly were the Beak brothers, by whose habits you could set a watch.

The door of Jim Beak's house opened as the church clock struck eight and Jim came out, wearing a blue blazer and carrying a mackintosh over his arm. On days when the rain was heavy he wore it. He had a brown oil-cloth bag in his other hand. His small blue car was parked in the lay-by opposite. By 8.03 the engine was running and by four minutes past, Jim Beak had driven out of the village.

Fern saw Norman Beak leave the loaf-shaped house as the church clock struck the half hour. He wore a sports jacket or occasionally a suit and carried a briefcase. He had neither mackintosh nor umbrella and when it was pouring with rain he ran to the lean-to that sheltered his car, with a newspaper held over his head. The paperboy delivered to Norman but not, Mary reported, to Jim.

After this, nothing happened, unless the cows were being moved or someone had a parcel delivery or, though this was quite rare, a visitor. There was nothing else to talk about and so they often talked about the Beaks, feeling both a rivalry yet also an odd sort of kinship with these other Irish twins.

Why don't they live in the same house? It would save money. Why were they not married? Had either of them ever had a wife and if so where was she? Where did they go to work every day?

They were not particularly imaginative children and so, although they sometimes thought of answers to their own questions, they were never very interesting answers and they lacked the romantic skill to invent fantasies and build remarkable stories around Jim and Norman Beak.

The grey wet weather ended and summer came, releasing them into the village and the fields and footpaths and copses and farmyards around about, and giving them long, sunlit days in which to find friends. Their father went back; the cottage door and windows stood open; and the whitewashed walls lifted Lou Piper's heart enough to encourage her to plant a few annuals in the back garden and then to sit outside in an old basket chair through the warm evenings, reading magazine stories and forgetting about the twins.

She had found out all there was to find, or so she thought, about Jim and Norman Beak but did not bother to tell her daughters, for what interest would it be to them? She was not to know that Mary and Fern had investigated both the Beak houses.

Their first opportunity, though they did not immediately see it as such, came when Jim Beak's cold water pipes had to be seen to by the plumber and, his neighbours on either side being unavailable, he had asked

Lou to keep the house keys. But Lou had been stricken with an abscessed tooth and gone to the town dentist, leaving the girls to hand the keys over.

"We won't," Mary had said, "we'll go up there and open the door for him – and look inside…"

"We can't."

"Why?"

They went. The job took the plumber over an hour, which gave them time to investigate everything thoroughly and then to sit on Jim Beak's sofa side by side, and wait.

The first thing they noticed was how little of anything there was in the house. Little furniture, mainly, but also little in the way of decorations – no ornaments, pictures, photographs. But when Fern opened a door leading into the larder, everything fell out. Beyond the back door were a scullery and an outhouse and then a garden shed, all of them crammed with things – utensils, old burnt saucepans, rusty chains, sets of scales and weights, bicycle wheels, bits of broken glass and china. Few of them seemed to be related to other bits. There were random sections of hosepipe, buckets, fire irons, carpet beaters, milk pails, broken fenders and half a spinning wheel. Dirt and dust and a dead rat and the frail bodies of mummified butterflies, along with a ton of dead flies, fell out together in the crash that brought the plumber.

"What...?"

But the sight of the girls' stricken faces, hands over their mouths, eyes huge and desperate, made him laugh. After he had helped them shove all the junk back and left, they stood in the hallway looking at each other and then Mary turned and headed up the stairs, Fern bleating out a protest but following nevertheless.

The first bedroom held a single bed and a chest of drawers. There was no carpet, only a rug. The back bedroom had a wooden trunk and a clothes horse and no rug.

There was nothing in the bathroom other than bath, basin and lavatory with a shaving brush and razor on the shelf, and one toilet roll.

"Doesn't he cut himself?" Fern whispered, for there was no mirror.

"Why are you whispering?" She did not know.

"We shouldn't be up here at all."

Jim Beak's house had told them not one single thing about him and yet it had told them everything, if they had been old enough to read the signs. They knew that he was a senior librarian – Lou had found that out.

"But there weren't any books." Fern said that night.

"I suppose he has enough of books all day."

It made sense.

They were not real twins and although they resembled

one another they were not identical and yet, perhaps as a result of having always been so much together, they often picked up on each other's thoughts and answered questions that were still unasked. When Fern said, "I wonder if the inside of Norman Beak's house is the same?" Mary had only to glance at her sister to know what was coming next.

"We couldn't."

"No," Fern said, "of course we couldn't."

It was some weeks since they had been inside Jim Beak's house.

He had come to collect the key that same evening and thanked them and given them a bar of milk chocolate, which Lou Piper said they should have refused. They had never told their mother about going inside but they talked sporadically between themselves, about the stuff that had fallen out of the cupboards, about the sparseness of the furnishings. They had wondered why but when, as usual, they could not think up any satisfactory answers, the topic had petered out. Life went on. They stood looking out of their windows less often.

They began to bring back heavy bags full of books from school and worked late at separate tables in their individual window spaces. Mary had an aptitude for languages; Fern was practical, liked science. Their subjects for the public exams chose themselves. They were neither clever nor dull. Their marks came in the middle. They were in different forms. There was nothing to single them out and who thought being Irish twins was of any importance? They had long stopped mentioning it.

The days closed in and they did not see the Beak brothers except by the lights of their cars as they returned home in the evenings, Jim at half past six, Norman twenty minutes later.

"They never visit one another," Mary said, looking up from a page of French translation.

"We don't know that, not for certain."

The year turned. They worked and took mock exams and got average, unremarkable results. The father they had seen so little of died in an accident and they were uncertain of their feelings, other than the temporary ones of shock and disorientation.

"No question of you going off to colleges now," Lou said.

"There has to be *some* way," Fern said.

"Of course we will go, we *have* to go," Mary said, picking up on her sister's meaning and suddenly, life in the village seemed suffocating and unbearable. They stared bleakly out of their windows, not knowing how they would ever manage to leave.

The next day they went for a despairing walk up the lane, past Jim Beak's cottage, along the track that skirted the back of the village and round in a half circle until they reached the field behind Norman's cottage. His car was not parked under the lean-to. Without speaking or even glancing at one another, they slipped round. A couple of stone steps led up from the scrubby garden to the back door and a row of windows. They hesitated. Here, the house was not overlooked at all.

Fern edged along to the first window, cupped her hands and peered in, but the window gave on to a small porch with nothing in it. Through the next window was the sitting room, which also had two windows opposite them, facing the front of the house. They both looked in for a long time.

"He leaves everything out," Fern said in the end.

Mary nodded. "Where Jim stores it away."

The room was as stuffed full of furniture and objects as any room could possibly be. A high backed settle, chairs, tables, two dressers, a cupboard, pictures, brass ornaments, a gong, clocks and china jugs, rugs and cushions. No inch of wall and barely any floor was left uncovered, everything was dark – dark polished oak, dark red and green leather covers, dark tapestry. The windows were grubby and let in little light.

The kitchen at the far end was small, dim and similarly full of crockery, china, utensils, vases, enamel bowls and jugs and rows of plants in pots. There was something derelict about the place, as if it had been left to gather dust and to rot for a hundred years.

"But he lives in it," Fern said. It was unimaginable. How could Norman Beak even tread a path between the tables and chairs and stools and fire screens?

They moved away in silence and a strange sort of awe, pitying a man who had to return alone every night to such a place. Jim went home to his own half-empty rooms, but they had not felt forbidding. However, they did not want to go inside the place they could see through Norman's window. It was like Miss Havisham's cobwebbed and crumbling room. They looked at one another and thought of mice and bats, of spiders and the ancient nests of wasps.

That summer changed everything. Mary's exam results were surprisingly good. She would enter the sixth form and perhaps gain a university scholarship. Fern, though she did not actually fail anything, only achieved bare passes in most subjects and low grades in the sciences at which she had apparently showed such promise. A tall poppy, she was scythed down and left to lie while the spotlight rested on her sister.

"I'm sorry," Mary kept on saying, for she could think of no words of consolation, but Fern stood at her window and would not turn to look at her sister.

For the first time in their lives, Fern separated herself and began to go about either with one or two new friends from nearby villages or by herself. Mary was puzzled and surprised but, ploughing her own furrow, was too inattentive to her sister to be hurt by her or to dwell on the changes.

The biggest change of all came about when, one Sunday afternoon, Mary went to the post box for her mother and found Jim Beak with one arm trapped in the bars of his front gate, having pushed it through trying to dislodge the jammed latch, twisting his arm in doing so. It was not painfully wedged but he had given up trying to extract it on his own when Mary stopped. With instructions from Jim, she found a small saw among the piles of scullery junk and sawed part of the gate off without difficulty – the wood was brittle, being rotten in its socket, and snapped easily.

"I'm glad to see you. Nobody was about; I don't know what I was going to do."

"Somebody would have come." But the street was deserted and every house closed in upon itself.

"I could have been there all night."

And perhaps he would, Mary had thought and then

for the first time she looked at Jim Beak directly, full in his face. He smiled at her and at once looked much younger.

"He's an Irish twin," Mary said some days later, after Fern had questioned and questioned her. "We have a bond."

"*We're* Irish twins," Fern said, "*we* have a bond."

"That's not the same."

They had never been so separate. Fern went for walks on her own and looked alone out of her window, to the other side of the village. Their positions were reversed. She started to work hard, Mary did no work at all. But if Fern had assumed that their mother would be full of disapproval and would make plans to put a stop to the relationship between her sister and Jim Beak, she was wrong. Lou seemed to be very happy, even encouraging. Jim Beak came to Sunday lunch and then to supper, twice within a couple of weeks.

"It's weird. It's peculiar, he's nearly fifty and don't say he doesn't look it because that's not the point," said Fern.

"So what is? He's a decent man, he's educated, he has a good job, he isn't married or separated or divorced, so what *is* wrong?"

Fern had no answer.

"You're jealous, of course."

Fern was not. She did not want to go out with a man more than so many years older and never leave this place, she wanted to go far away, start a new life entirely of her own. She was working towards it. Yet she felt as if a limb had been cut off. She was lonely. 'Irish twin' meant nothing after all. Mary had gone from being her sister, friend, companion, the one who picked up on Fern's thoughts before she had even spoken them and completed her half-finished sentences, to being a stranger who happened to share her room (Mary never spent a night at Jim Beak's). She slipped off a skin, to reveal a person who had new ideas and views, dressed differently, even seemed to have changed her voice and her gestures. She was not unfriendly or unloving, she simply seemed unaware of Fern altogether. Fern felt herself to be invisible, like a ghost, desperately trying to communicate with someone in the old life and unable to get through but forced to remain unseen, unheard.

Fern slept badly, she had headaches and once or twice terrifying random attacks of panic when she reached out to Mary for support – but there was no Mary, only space and empty air. She found it difficult to concentrate on work. She was asked, quite kindly, if she had any personal problems and said no. Her ambition faltered. Oxbridge faded from her thoughts, which for a short time turned to some new university, less prestigious, before she lost her nerve altogether and could not bear the thought of going away from home. Mary noticed nothing. Lou never had.

The wedding was in July.

"What am I wearing?" Fern was quite thin now and hoped the bridesmaid's dress would conceal her bony shoulders.

"Whatever you like. You didn't think you were being a bridesmaid? I'm having Annie Green's little sister, and that's all."

Fern flushed, feeling embarrassed and foolish at having assumed it.

She did not do well enough in her exams to take up even a modest university place. At school they suggested re-takes or a gap year and were still sympathetic, still puzzled.

"You can talk to me in confidence, Fern," said her head teacher, "if you have personal issues."

But where would she begin?

Mary and Jim Beak went to the Lake District for their honeymoon.

"When they come back," Lou said, "you can't just go dropping in. Wait until you're invited."

Fern went out late for walks and once it was dark crept to the back of the Beaks' house and tried to see through their windows. Once or twice, Mary was in the kitchen, at the stove or the sink. She looked the same but she was not the same and how did she know how to cook and look after a house? She had walked over to pull the curtains and Fern shrank back into the bushes, terrified of being seen and how it would look, what her sister might say.

After a while she edged forwards again to peer through a chink and saw her lying full-length on the sofa, reading a book. Nothing looked different. There was no more furniture. Fern wondered if junk still fell out of every cupboard when the door was opened.

The following spring, Fern re-took three exams but did no better.

"You'll have to do something," Lou said. "Look for a job. I can't afford to keep you."

At night, Fern lay awake and missed Mary, as if she were five years old again. Her sister lived a hundred yards away and it might have been in another country.

"*Dear Mary – I have to talk to you. I have to get a job. Can you think of anything? Can you come down and see me?*"

She slipped the note under the door after she had seen

the two of them go off in the car one Saturday afternoon.

She won't care. She will care. She has to come. She won't come.

"Why didn't you just knock?" Mary said, opening the door the next day to put out the milk bottles, and seeing her sister walking past. "What's wrong with you? You're not bothered by Jim are you?"

Fern felt all the words she might have spoken harden and become pebbles in her mouth.

"Have you sorted through everything in the cupboards yet?'

They sat at the kitchen table with mugs of tea. It was hard to accept that Mary was still her sister, that this was where she lived now.

"Oh no, I won't bother. Anyway, that's Jim's department."

"But what does he intend to do with it all?"

"Nothing, so far as I can tell."

"Doesn't it bother you?"

"No. Why would it?"

"Don't you want any new stuff?"

"Nothing wrong with what there is. We don't need it. Well – we bought new towels, and a bath mat."

"What do you do?"

"Read. Talk. Do the garden. Jim grows everything.

We're getting some chickens." Fern stirred her tea and stared at it, going round and round like a small brown whirlpool. All the things she wondered about and that troubled her could not be mentioned.

"What can I do, Mary? I have to do something."

"What happened to you, Fern?"

Fern stared. You, she wanted to say, you happened. This happened. What you did. You.

She shrugged. "Would Jim know of anything?"

"Jim is a librarian. You don't know anything about libraries."

"No."

"I suppose Norman might. You could try him."

"I've never spoken to Norman. Not really."

She tried to remember if they had exchanged any word at all at the wedding.

"Well, he won't bite you. If there was any lab job going, say, he might know."

"Would Jim ask him for me?"

"Ask him yourself. I've got to get ready to go out now, Fern."

"Where to?"

"Mind your own beeswax."

But she came over and put her arm around Fern's shoulders.

"Come on."

"It isn't the same now, Mary."

"Of course it isn't. I'm married, that's all."

Fern turned away.

"Better look to marrying yourself, put us on an equal footing again," Mary called at the door.

"We're Irish twins, you can't alter that Mary."

"Oh, for heaven's sake. That means nothing. Never did really. What do you think?"

But she had always thought, and so had Mary, she knew it, she knew it, that it had meant everything.

She watched the clock. Ten, fifteen, twenty minutes. Half-an-hour.

"Where are you going off to now?" asked Lou.

"Not far."

"Well don't, and if you're later than seven it'll go cold."

Norman's hair was receding a bit. He had a slight stammer – more of a speech hesitation.

"Fern? Hell...hello."

She had returned to the bottom step once she had rung the bell, so that he was looking down on the top of her head.

"C...come in." But he did not hold the door open any wider.

"Am I bothering you? Are you having your supper?"

"No. Pl… please. Come in."

The front door opened straight into the long main room and at first she could not see anything, it was so dark.

"So sorry. Sorry."

There was a table lamp that gave off a very dim light as it tried to force itself through a waxen-looking shade. There was an aura of darkness from the heavy furniture, the oak sideboard, dresser, tables, chairs, wall cabinets, clock, the dark brown leather sofa, the red Turkish carpet and rug, the black grate, the carved mantelpiece lined with brass ornaments. Fern stood wondering how she might pick her way through to a seat.

But he did not ask her to sit down.

"I'm afraid mother kept everything like this and I never quite got round to changing anything."

"It's very nice."

She knew that his mother had been dead for sixteen years.

"Can I get you anything? Or – no…?"

"No thank you. I just came to ask – it was Mary's idea."

He stood smiling at her uncertainly in the dim room, which smelled of old things and the absence of sunlight.

How can he live like this? How could he not have

cleared anything at all out, changed anything, moved anything, for sixteen years?

Norman had gentle eyes and very white hands.

He listened.

"The problem would be, Fern, training. You have had no training."

"No."

"An interest then?"

"Oh yes."

"Perhaps you could do a course. But lab assistant jobs are – well – thin on the ground and rather poorly paid too, I'm afraid. We are very conscious of that. And as for prospects – it isn't easy. No it isn't easy."

"I see. Well, thank you anyway."

"But of course, if anything – if...'

She went quickly, her face hot, not looking back but feeling his presence behind her, feeling his eyes following her as she went up the lane.

Perhaps the idea had formed itself long ago. Norman looked younger than Jim, in spite of the receding hair. If nothing else, he needed someone to help him clear out the house. She thought about the pictures on the dark walls and the great speckled mirror. She could hardly go back on some pretext, because what pretext could there be?

A few days later he called, stopping the car outside their house on his way back from work. He had a card folder, full of information leaflets about training courses and diplomas and career paths. He stood on the doorstep, his skin faintly grubby. A chemical smell came off his clothes.

"Come in, Norman, don't stand there outside, come in – stay to tea, there's plenty." Lou almost seemed to shake with eagerness. They did not expect him to accept. It was cottage pie and frozen peas. A bottle of sherry came out from the depths of the cupboard, left over from the wedding. Fern did not know whether to be pleased or horrified and tried to show nothing.

"We should see more of you. We see little enough of Mary and Jim, heaven knows yet we all live within spitting distance. And you're family now."

"I suppose I am. Yes."

"And this is a friendly village."

"Quite friendly," Norman said, wiping his mouth on the paper napkin. It was white and silver, also left over from the wedding.

"Of course, mother knew everyone."

"I'm thinking she came here when she was married?"

"No, no, she was born here. In... in the house. So were we. Her brother was the one who moved in later – into Jim's cottage. When he died he left it to Jim."

"So you all lived together at one time?"

"But then… and Jim fancied a place of his own which was somewhat of a surprise …" Norman stood up. "This has been very nice, Mrs Piper, an unexpected treat. Thank you."

Lou looked across at Fern, a look that meant something but exactly what Fern could not tell.

"Thank you very much for getting all these," Fern said, touching the folder. "It was very kind of you."

"Only too pleased, only too pleased."

She realised how often he said things twice.

"A very nice man," Lou said, "a very nice man."

Fern read carefully through the brochures and sheets of information and found that she could qualify as a laboratory assistant in several ways, the best being on-the-job, with daily release at a college. But there were no jobs, Norman had said, at least not at the moment, on the science campus where he worked.

"Why would you want to do that?" She had come to see Mary, hoping to get her out for a walk, in the old way, but Mary was waiting for things in the oven.

"I liked the practical things, science."

"Yes. Well."

"Norman likes it."

"That's different."

"Why is it?"

"Norman is in a senior position. He runs a team. You would only be a dogsbody."

But then Mary took hold of her sister's shoulders and turned her around, looking hard into her face.

"You like Norman, don't you?"

Fern could not reply, in spite of knowing what the question meant.

"You needn't have brought these, I didn't want them back."

Fern stood on the doorstep awkwardly, holding the folder.

"Please keep them, Fern. I have no use for them."

Norman had taken his tie off and his shirt was open at the neck, showing a black tuft of dark hair. There was a slightly lemon scent coming from him.

"I would ask you in but I'm afraid I'm getting ready to go out to the theatre with some colleagues from work."

Fern took a step back and almost fell.

"*The Importance of Being Earnest*. Amateurs I'm afraid, but one of my colleagues has a part in it."

The grandfather clock chimed inside the house. She remembered having seen it in the front room. It had a dial with the moon and stars in faded blues and gold.

"That was my mother's favourite," Norman said, listening. "It keeps good time. Thomas Tompion."

"The friend in the play?"

He blinked, half smiled, but did not make her feel foolish when he said, "The man who made the clock. Come and have tea one day or a glass of wine. My home-made wine. Like Thomas I suppose." He smiled again. He had gentle eyes. "He made the clock, I make the wine."

"Well –" Fern almost tripped over again as she turned away.

"Those steps." Norman said, shaking his head. "Those steps need some attention."

But she had gone out of ear-shot, back into the lane.

A life beyond the loaf-shaped cottage crammed full of old furniture, one in which Norman had work colleagues and went to the theatre, seemed both exciting and difficult to picture and she spent a long time trying to work it out, to decide if these people were men, women, or both, his age, younger or older, what they wore and talked about, what kind of houses they might live in and who with and exactly where. Not in this place. Like Jim, Norman Beak had always kept home and his other life apart. They had been born here and returned to it but in between they must have both gone away to yet other worlds. Mary had told her that Jim went to university in

Edinburgh. She wasn't sure about Norman, she said, and she would ask. But it was never mentioned again.

"I thought you might be interested, Fern. I've been making enquiries, you know, putting out feelers, and I heard today – there may be a training post coming up soon – well, in a month or so."

"In your labs?"

"Well, no – no. We are fully-staffed I'm afraid, but – in the chemical engineering schools on the other side of the campus. It could be an interesting opening. Potentially."

Norman stood leaning on the car door. The late sun picked out a bald patch at the back of his head. His hair was usually combed over it carefully.

"What should I do?"

"Nothing, nothing at all, as of now. If there is anything I would nudge you, so to speak. But I thought you might like to know that these opportunities do arise." He started to get back into the car.

"Can I get you a cup of tea or anything, Norman?" It was the first time she had used his name to his face. It felt daring.

"Ah, thank you Fern but I'm going out almost at once. Meeting some work colleagues for an early supper."

Did he not see enough of these work colleagues at work? Was this how it would be?

"They are going to tell me all about my holiday destination – these friends have been twice you see and it always pays to find out everything you can, don't you agree? Before going to any foreign country."

Fern had never been to any foreign country. She smiled vaguely.

"How long will you be away?"

"Three weeks. Not until May though."

"I'm afraid I have absolutely no idea," Mary said, in the airy way she had cultivated since marrying Jim. "We don't see much of Norman."

"But he only lives down the lane."

"Yes."

"And he and Jim are Irish twins."

Mary turned away with a click of her tongue.

"That means nothing."

"Doesn't it mean anything to you, that we are?"

"I wish you'd grow up, Fern. Listen, I'll make coffee for us but then you will have to go; you can't just come and sit around here all day. When does this course start, anyway?"

"I'm not sure."

The click again.

"Does he always go abroad on holiday?"

"I just said, I've no idea."

"For the sun, I suppose. Or maybe it's one of those 'interest holidays'. I can imagine him going to different places and hearing lectures about them or about something else. History or art may be. Can't you?"

"I don't see why it's of the slightest interest."

"It isn't."

Mary put down the sugar bowl and looked hard at her sister across the kitchen table whose wood had faded blonde with so many years of scrubbing. The Beaks did not seem either to throw away or to replace anything if there were a breath of life left in it.

"Now look, Fern –"

Fern did not meet her sister's eye.

"Look – you're not –?"

They were both silent. The kitchen clock ticked. Old clocks, old clocks. Neither of them spoke. Neither needed to. Everything that might or could or would never be said lay heavy in the air between them, as it used to do. It worked still. They each knew what the other was thinking and so words were unnecessary.

* * *

The day after Norman went away a letter came from the Chemical Engineering Department. '*A trainee lab assistant with two days a week college release – her name had been put forward – if she wanted to register an interest – if she would please fill in…*'

Fern did not know if she had an interest. But she couldn't hang about the village doing nothing, waiting for Norman. If he were here she would have an excuse for calling at the house to ask his advice, and it occurred to her that if she did get the trainee post, she could travel in every day with him. What reason would he have to refuse?

They would let her know within a week, they said, after showing her and six others round the labs, which were situated in a concrete block. No one working there looked up at them or spoke. No one talked to anyone else. The science campus was windswept and flat.

But if she succeeded, none of that would signify, because each morning and evening she would travel in Norman's car. What happened between would simply be time filled in.

Warnings nudged their way into the corner of her mind and slipped into her last thoughts at night. Fern ignored them and knew that she was ignoring them and occasionally felt anxious, but brushed the anxiousness aside. She told no one, talked to no one. But of course Mary knew.

Two or three times she went out late at night, when it was warm and she could find her way round to the back of the loaf-shaped house by the bright moon. She cupped her hands and looked in through the windows and saw the darkly crowded room and the face of the grandfather clock and then saw herself in there and the sight was right and fitting. There would be no need to change anything or move or remove it either. She would make a living addition to it, that was all. A completion.

She slipped back up the lane, and in bed lay awake, picturing it all, as the moon silvered her bed cover and in a confused and drowsy second, she turned to tell her Irish twin that she knew she would marry Norman Beak.

A couple of days before he was due home again, Fern had felt unwell, then in pain, then in extreme pain. The ambulance took her to hospital to have her appendix removed, as an emergency. An infection kept her there. Mary came, white-faced.

"We thought you were going to die," she said and held her hand very tightly. "I was really scared, Fern."

Fern felt so weak that she might have cried at anything but after Mary had gone that evening she cried as she had not done since she was five or six years old, overwhelmed with the knowledge that her sister did love her, did care about her and had never entirely gone away from her.

Jim drove Mary over after he got back from work, never missing a day.

"You're my sister – your Jim's sister-in-law – why ever

wouldn't he? He was afraid too, that you were going to die."

It was Jim and Mary who came to fetch her home. The world seemed to be in a mad rush. Traffic moved too fast. Fern closed her eyes, afraid of everything.

"Nearly home."

She opened her eyes, to see the church and the lane leading down from it. It was drizzling and the village was shrouded in mist. Everywhere looked strange and nothing mattered.

"Is Norman back home?" Fern said. "Did he have a good holiday in the sun?'

She caught a quick glance between Mary and Jim. But then Jim was helping her with great care from the car and Lou was at the door.

"Lean on me, that's it," Jim said. Fern felt dizzy.

In her room, which she reached slow step after slow step, resting in between each one, she saw a jug of cottage flowers, with a card propped in front of it and at once she was sure they had come from Norman.

"Show me," she said, when Mary had helped her undress and get into bed. Mary reached down the card.

"Everyone signed it," she said, "I went round – and Jim went to one or two."

The whole village had written inside the card, even people Fern barely knew and a few only recently moved in. Fern's eyes ran down the list until she found it. Norman (Beak).

Immediately beneath that someone else had signed their name, in capital letters, like a child learning to write: 'MRS NORMAN BEAK'.

Fern felt the blood flush up through her body and suffuse her face. Her scalp prickled. Mary's eyes shifted from her to the window and from the window to the wall.

"Oh that," she said, "Did I not tell you?"

Neither of them could talk about it. Neither knew how such a conversation could start. So much had been left unsaid from the beginning – but the beginning of what?

"The elephant in the room," Jim said that night. "It's the perfect example." He turned the page of his newspaper. "Mind you –" he looked across at Mary. "I have never been able to work him out. My brother."

Perhaps for the first time, Mary knew what he meant.

It was another three weeks before Fern had the strength or the will to go out. The infection had flared up again, sending her back to hospital for a night. It rained and the sky was like the inside of a saucepan, day after day. She lay dozing, sometimes reading, and Mary came down every morning and they talked about anything. But not about that.

The day the sun shone after weeks of rain and sepia skies, Fern went to find out, whatever there was to find and whatever way she could. Lou had gone off to her Wednesday cleaning job. At half past ten in the morning there would be no one about in the village. Perhaps no one at all in the loaf-shaped house.

But there was. The door and all the windows were wide open. There was a large skip in the front, piled high with an old sofa, a side table, a bed frame. Three or four pictures leaned against it, with a wicker basket full of china and glass. A couple of old Turkish carpets lay on the grass.

Fern stood, unable to work out what was happening. Norman's car was not there. She wondered if he was spring-cleaning, moving or just clearing out things that were broken, had holes or were rotten – as most of the things she had seen herself had been. Nothing had been looked after, or repaired, Mary had said, since the Beaks' mother had died and most probably for years before that.

And then a woman came out of the house. She was carrying a large mirror, the glass was spotted over, the frame cracked and tarnished. Fern remembered having seen it on the sitting room wall.

"Good morning?"

She was small and slender, with shining black hair, very like the few other Filipino women Fern had seen.

She was neither plain nor pretty and it was impossible to tell her age. Fern's throat constricted but the woman set down the mirror and came to her, holding out her slender hand. It had a child's fingers.

"I am Mrs Norman Beak." They stood uncertainly, Fern looking past the woman to the furniture.

"Yes, it is all to go, all to clear out. Everything. So much old broken things. But Norman says to clear out anything, everything. What I want, don't want and then – new kitchen, new bath, new modern chairs and tables, new paint and pictures. Everything. Tomorrow," she waved at the skip, "all to go. Then next lot until everything gone. Would you like a cup of tea?"

Fern managed to shake her head, mutter something unintelligible, and go.

"Mrs Norman Beak," the sweetly-tuned voice came after her. Mrs Norman Beak.

"I swear to you we didn't know. He didn't say a word to a soul beforehand, I swear to you, Fern. Well, not to us at any rate. He went out there to look for a wife and he found one. All I know is that she wanted to clear all the old stuff out and he said yes. He even got a valuer, he wanted to auction it all. The man said it would have been worth a small fortune if it had not been in such bad condition – rotten, a lot of it, the only things still worth anything were the Crown Derby tea set and the grandfather clock, but apparently she wants to keep those. Jim's livid. If they were never great friends before, it's a stand-off now. Jim won't speak to him."

"I don't understand. Why has he brought her here? He could have…"

Mary looked at her with an odd tenderness. "No," she said, "it wouldn't have done."

"Why not?"

She knew that Mary had no answer, that there was no good reason why not and yet every reason.

She thought of Mrs Norman Beak – slight, dainty, with her tiny waist and feet.

The loaf-shaped cottage was emptied and builders moved in. Fern tried to picture it with a shining new kitchen and bathroom, bright tiles and dazzling white walls and the grandfather clock standing like a great-bodied, awkward old man, out of place in the middle of it all.

She tried to avoid Norman and mostly succeeded. But when she started her trainee job, she stood at the bus stop as he went past every morning. They were going in the same direction, just to two different parts of the campus. She would have gone in with him. It had all been planned, but now he drove past her in his new car, too embarrassed, too awkward – who knew? – to acknowledge her, with the girl-wife sitting beside him, dark, shining hair pulled back from her exquisite little face.

Mrs Norman Beak.

Fern wondered whether he had told her about being an Irish twin and decided that he had not. It seemed to mean nothing to him. Nothing to any of them, apart from her. Nothing at all.

CRYSTAL

CRYSTAL

Shelagh. Eileen. Bernadette. Annie. Clare, and Catherine. John.

She had given up hope by then but from the first moment Mary Maguire knew his destiny, as they all did and fully understood. John, the son, the gift she had to give back.

He would have been a mother's boy except that there were six other females wanting to share him. Joe Maguire mostly kept out of it but his ear was to the ground and he sometimes feared for his son, who was short and black haired and so pale of skin he was always thought to be ill. But John was never ill, he was thin and strong as a peeled branch.

'Forgive me father, for I have sinned. This is my first confession.'

The priest's ear pressed to the grille.

'I wouldn't want to do that,' John had said later. His mother was close by the window to catch the last light, peering at the lapel of his new jacket for fear of the slightest mark.

'What's that you wouldn't want?'

'Listen to people telling their sins, not when I knew who they were. I wouldn't want to do that.'

She slipped a wooden hanger through the jacket sleeves. The girls had each had a new lace veil for their First Communions though the dress had been handed down. No one expected any different. But money was naturally found for John's new jacket and that was expected too.

It was spring. The window was open a chink and the air coming in had the musty smell of May blossom.

'God makes sure the priest forgets what he's been told the very second he leaves the confessional.'

She knew everything.

When Ma had gone, he lay watching the darkness soak up through the cotton curtains like a stain. The curtains were his soul and the stain was of sin. And what if she was wrong and the priest remembered, even just one thing he'd been told?

Years later, in the concrete city, he thought of that night and the worry of it and in the confessional he himself wanted to reassure any child on the other side of the grille that he would not remember what was being said to him. God saw to that.

From birth the purpose of his life had been mapped out for him and the way known and it did not occur to him to question anything. He might kick at the wall that stood in front of him, but he never questioned what he was meant to do.

The years of scratching letters with a stone on the back step, of playground football and slipping the white altar boy's surplice over his head each Sunday were one continuous seam of time and then he was leaning against the wall with three or four others, smoking and watching people go into the Friday night dance. He could not dance. He had never wanted to learn to dance. He had football feet not dancing feet.

He watched a giggle of girls in full skirts go up the steps into the Castle Hotel.

Someone shoved him. 'Eyes down, John Maguire.'

'Geddof will you!'

A couple of them laughed because he flushed up straight away, he felt his skin burn and wanted to disappear with shame.

In two weeks' time he would make the journey of seventy miles, to the Seminary.

'Go on then, get in there why don't you?'

One girl in bright red and all petticoats beneath glanced at him under her eyelashes but when he looked harder, seemed not to be glancing in any way at all.

He dropped the cigarette stub and crushed it under his heel and the picture came straight into his mind as it always would, of the slender plaster foot of the Virgin in the church, crushing the head of the serpent.

On the following Tuesday, he had walked into the house and there was the same girl, the one who had looked and then not looked, sitting at the table with Clare and Ma poring over some dress pattern that was spread out on the oilcloth. Shelagh and Eileen were married by now and in their own places and Bernadette gone for nursing, leaving Mary, Clare and Catherine only at home. Clare was the social one. She was seventeen. Her friends were always in and out. But this one he had never seen, this one was new.

She looked up and not under her eyelashes this time but directly at him.

'It's just my brother John,' Clare said.

She still looked at him. 'I know,' she said. But did not offer her own name in return.

'I'll leave you two to pin this together, I've to make the tea. John you'll have reading to do.'

'No,' he said. The girl had hair so dark as to be almost

black. Gleaming. The red dress had been just the right one.

'John?'

Ma had eyes in the back of her head. Ma could see through walls. Ma knew everything.

He went upstairs.

He had no right even to look at a girl, no matter if she was his sister's friend, he was to be a priest, off to the seminary in two weeks. He had a picture of himself walking round the garden reading his breviary, wearing the black soutane, silent, his hair chopped short. He longed to go. He had longed since the idea had first been seeded inside his head. He was chosen, Ma said.

He had no right to look at a girl.

He went back downstairs and looked. Clare was out of the room, Ma in the scullery.

'Hello again John,' she said.

'What's your name?'

She turned then, half way, a glance over her shoulder. 'Cecilia.'

'I've an Aunt Cecilia.'

'I know that.'

Before he knew he would say it he said, 'Would you come for a walk?'

Joe returned from work and Ma served his tea first, as

always, then sat at the table with the rest of them. Clare, John. Cecilia. The bread and butter swelled in his mouth like greasy cotton wool and his throat would not close on it, he had to shove it down painfully with scalding tea. Then the cake went to clumps of sawdust and stuck to the roof of his mouth.

He should not have spoken to her and the sin burned up inside him and yet never burned out, and consumed nothing, as is the way of sin.

Only once she looked at him, the glance under her lashes, and then turned her head and whispered something to Clare, who smiled…

'Would you come for a walk?' he had asked, without any idea how they might do it but to Cecilia it presented no problem. She said goodnight after she had helped clear the tea table and done a bit more on the dress, and just looked at him as she closed the door. He waited five minutes. Joe was asleep with the paper in front of his face, Ma and Clare worked at pinning the pattern onto some flowery material.

He just went out. No one glanced up or even noticed.

Outside there was a band of enamel blue light left in the sky.

She was standing at the corner.

'Do you have a cigarette?'

At the end of the next street was a small paddock with a couple of horses in it and they leaned their backs on the fence there. He lit their cigarettes.

'You're going to the seminary then.'

His life went upside down like an egg timer with the sand dropping straight to the pit of his stomach.

'Well, I don't know.'

'You should. You can't go there and not know.'

He looked at his feet but it had gone quite dark now and he could not see them, he only saw the faint gleam of her cheekbone and the burning red tips of their cigarettes.

You can't go there and not know.

No.

'I've always been going there,' he said. 'It's a vocation.'

'Your own or your Ma's?'

He wondered how she dared to say that. How she knew.

'You'll come back a priest then.'

'No, no, not for a long while. I'll come back for holidays just a seminarian.'

'It sets you apart.'

He knew it. Ma said he had been set apart from the beginning, as the boy after six girls.

'We could go for a drink if you'd like,' he said.

One of the horses came ambling across and leaned

its great head between them. Its breath blew warm and damp on the back of his neck.

'I used to have a pony,' Cecilia said.

'Ah. I never did.'

'So – should we go for a drink?'

'I like it here. Just talking.' She stroked the soft hairy muzzle of the horse.

'Yes.'

He finished his cigarette and crushed it under his foot and the image was there again, lit by blazing rings of candles, the pale plaster foot of the Virgin, the serpent's head, forever waiting to be crushed.

'I have to go,' he said. 'I shouldn't be here.' He was suddenly faint with the guilt of it.

He felt her look at him, just once, and then she was gone and he was alone with the horse, blowing the warmth from its nostrils onto his cheek.

He went to bed expecting to dream about Cecilia but he dreamed nothing and he did not see her again until he went away and after that life changed so entirely and he with it that he never thought about her either.

He had one moment, perhaps less, perhaps only the moment's shadow, when he panicked and thought he was not doing what he himself wanted or going the way that was right for him, and he might have run then.

They were waiting for Liam's taxi that would take him the twelve miles to the railway station, with as many of them crammed into their front room as could manage to get there – Joe, Ma, five of the girls, the next door neighbours, his best friend Anthony Kerrigan. And looking round at them, their faces set, Ma crying, and Clare and Catherine too, no one wanting to meet his eye, it seemed as if they were waiting for the hearse that was to take him to his grave. He could not breathe for all their bodies in the room and it was then that he almost ran.

But Liam's taxi horn parped outside and the chance was gone, if he had ever wanted to take it. He could not have said. He peered to right and left as they drove away, wondering if Cecilia might have come to see him off, even just to wave from the distance. But he caught no glimpse of her and then they were rattling round the end of the street and away.

'You're different,' Clare said when he walked back into the house four months later and he felt it himself. Nothing had changed though the rooms seemed somehow smaller after the high ceilings and long corridors of the seminary. But it was in himself, he was set apart now and at last his vocation burned within him. He would not be a priest for some years but they treated him as one, Ma especially, elevating him to some place of her own making above them all, even above Joe now. Ma would look at him in wonder across the table.

He had put on his old grey sweater and the cords he liked. 'I somehow think you shouldn't wear those.'

'Why not? I feel right in these. I'm at home.'

She said no more, only shook her head but he knew she could not elevate him and see him as set apart if he wore the old grey sweater and cords just as before.

To make up for it, he said Latin grace before supper and gave a benediction after. Only Clare gave him a straight look. Nothing got past Clare.

'I'll take anyone who wants it for a glass of beer.'

'You won't go to the Club, John surely not?'

'I think I will.'

In Ma's youth it would never have been allowed.

'Times change,' John said.

Though not in many respects.

He could not sleep that night. He was used to the sounds of footsteps and voices and doors closing and last bells as everyone settled down, and to a less comfortable bed and the faint smell of varnish from a new chair. He had had no trouble getting used to it all and when the full realisation of where he was and why had come upon him, after a couple of weeks, he had been in awe of what his life was to be. Until then he had gone along with the plans of others but now it was his own way and he was sure the plan was the plan of God.

He had gone to the chapel and prayed in a great fervour.

And so his time went on. There was a great deal more study than he had expected and he had never been comfortable poring for hours over books. He looked up from his desk sometimes, out of the tall library windows onto the green meadow that sloped up to a crown of trees, and he felt stifled and wanted to run out into the open air to clear his head of words.

He made friends, none close, and as time went on, felt even more set apart, so that when he went home now it was quite natural for him to accept that his mother meant him to be on the pedestal she had made for him and stay there. Joe said little but there was pride in his gait when the two walked down through the town together and when others stood aside for him and bought him a beer at the bar of the Club. Old school friends kept just a little apart, even Anthony Kerrigan, who was married now and with a boy of his own.

Only Clare was the same, gave him no quarter, teased him, looked him straight in the eye though out of them all Clare loved him the most. They were left alone one afternoon and took the old bicycles out into the country and sat plaiting grasses on the edge of a field.

'Cecilia asked after you the other day,' she said, pulling another handful of the long, wiry stalks that bent the best. 'You remember Cecilia.'

'Oh yes. She had nearly black hair.'

'Like your own.' Clare gave him a look. 'Do you think about her?'

'About Cecilia? No, why would I?'

And he never had. He might not have remembered her at all but because Clare had mentioned her, she came vividly to mind, and the night he had stood with her by the paddock, the head of the horse, its warm breath, the red tips of their cigarettes.

'Anthony married Ruthie Nolan.'

'I know that, don't I?'

'Did you see their boy?'

'I did not.' He twirled a plaited grass between his finger and thumb.

'Are you happy there, John? Look me in the eyes.'

He did so and said that yes, he was, because that was the honest truth.

'Fine,' Clare said. 'Where will they send you?'

'I hope I might come down this way. There's two or three parishes will be needing a curate before long. But it could be that I'll have to go further, just at first. I'd like it if I could come back home soon.'

'They never allow it.'

'They might. It just all depends what God has in mind.'

'God and the Archbishop.'

He laughed. Clare did not.

But three years on, God and the Archbishop had England in mind. He was ordained in the July and had a month's holiday at home, when he celebrated Mass in his own parish and Ma walked a foot above the ground. He had earned his place on the pedestal she had made.

The line of those he knew went along the whole altar rail time after time, his family, the nephews and nieces, with the youngest ones being brought up for just his blessing, boys he had been at school with, men now with families.

And then, at the far end, he saw the bent head of shining black hair under the square of lace. He was in front of her before he knew it. Cecilia. For a second, the ground tipped at his feet so that he almost stumbled but it was only one second and he had given her the communion and moved away, to start the new row of people kneeling.

They had a huge lunch in the Castle Hotel, taking up an entire long table, as they had done at the family weddings, and the next of those would be Catherine, engaged now. Only Clare was left. Clare and John.

For the next two weeks, while Ma got him ready to the last sock and handkerchief, he kept mostly to the house, other than visiting his sisters and their families, all of whom had stayed in the town. He went to the Club with Joe. He tried not to look to right or left or over his shoulder, for fear of finding Cecilia there. His vocation still burned inside him. He offered up his life and all his strength and devotion to God, in his daily Mass, he longed to make a start on his future.

He did not see her at all until his last day. He had said he did not want anyone to see him off but the night before, when Clare came in, he changed his mind and asked her.

'I'll come all the way to the ferry with you. You should have someone to look back to.'

'Only don't tell Ma,' he said.

She left the house like a shadow and waited on the corner for Liam's taxi to pick her up after John.

'Do you see Cecilia now?' he asked as they were on the outskirts of the town.

His sister turned her face full towards him but he kept looking out of the window.

The ferry was not crowded and the day was fine and clear so that he could lean on the rail and watch the dock and the coastline, and Clare, fade and grow small as the smooth grey sea came between them. He did not feel a pang even for her, the one he was closest to, because he was full of the future and God's intentions for him. The flutter in the pit of his stomach was like the day before a holiday. But this was not to be a holiday, he would have the care of souls. This was his life.

He did not know what he expected and had not bothered to try and make up any picture of the place in his mind, for it was bound to be quite different but he had some idea of smoke and grime and chimneys and narrow streets between tall blackened houses.

The parish priest had written that he should get a taxi from the railway station until he knew his whereabouts. 'And you have your suitcase.' His case was not very heavy, he had only clothes, and his few books, bits and pieces, but he allowed himself the taxi, for a last pleasure and from obedience.

The priest was Fr Ryan.

The city was largely rebuilt since the war and there were no chimneys, no blackened walls, no grime but instead, there was concrete, in squares and towers and lines of houses, until they got a little way out of the centre when streets of pebble dash and brick and a bungalow here and there began. But a cinema and a bank and a factory were concrete, with an estate of grey concrete flats, a concrete school. The taxi wound in and out, swung right, swung left. The driver slowed down, bent forward, peered out.

'Here.'

The Presbytery. But it was no different from the other houses on the wide road.

Grey porridge front, black wooden gate, bow windows top and bottom. Short gravel path.

He was always to remember that, as he stood looking at it for the first time a terrible greyness seeped over him and he wanted to stop the taxi as it turned in the road, get back into it and run. He had never felt such a pain of longing to run back home in his life, not even when he had been on the steps of the cottage hospital as a small boy, going in to have the tonsils pulled out of his throat.

He turned to find the taxi gone. Until he had calmed himself he lit a cigarette and looked at the houses, thinking that this was home, this was what he must get used to every morning, every night, and the people in them, the church further back on the same road. The cigarette helped him feel the ground beneath his feet again and he smoked it right to the end and almost burnt his fingers. He had bought a big pack of them on the ferry…

It was a woman who opened the door, small, thin, grey.

'You'll be Father John.'

The hall smelled of cooking potatoes. She showed him to his room and the bathroom opposite, then left.

He looked out of the window. It had a view of the next-door house and a corner of the garden where two boys were swinging from a rope tied to a branch, swinging and jumping down, swinging and jumping down, and laughing. Laughing.

There was a front room which served for the dining room. There was the back sitting room. There was a small room to the side which was Father Ryan's study.

'You've a desk in your own room unless you need anything bigger? Father Barry never did.'

Father Ryan had come in just before seven, when they ate, gammon and peas and boiled potatoes, and tinned peaches with Carnation milk. Tea.

'You smoke cigarettes?' Father Ryan had gone in search of an ashtray and found one the size of a florin.

'Do you mind it, Father?'

'I never took to it myself.'

He was thin but with a pot belly, frameless spectacles, small eyes.

They ate almost in silence, the housekeeper fetching and carrying the dishes in silence as well. After grace, he said 'I will say the eight o'clock Mass, tomorrow, you will take the evening, there's the Parish to go round and the school. People to meet. You should get a good night's sleep, we work hard here Father. But I've something to show you first.'

John remembered the moment when the door to the sitting room was opened and the lights switched on, it stayed with him intact and whole, like a still life or an image from a film, even after everything was long over.

There was little to remark upon in the room itself. A settee, two armchairs, a bureau, a coffee table. The crucifix. A copy of the great painting, the Virgin with St Anne.

But along the back wall was a row of shelves and in front of them a sideboard, completely filled with crystal, displayed as if these were the crown jewels – bowls, vases, glasses, dishes, plates, cups, jugs, all of lead crystal, carved and faceted and patterned, every size, every shape.

Father Ryan went over and began to touch and caress piece after piece, turning this or that a little way, adjusting a bowl so that it caught the light better, moving a vase an inch or two. The crystal glinted on his spectacles.

'I would ask you to be very careful if you ever come in this room when I'm not here –and never to touch it, do you understand me?'

John could think of not a word to say. The crystal seemed an obscene thing, arrogant and gaudy as some glittering, gaudy evil. How the man had come by it all, whether he had been given it or left it in some will or simply bought it himself over years, he could not guess.

Father Ryan turned and behind the spectacles his small eyes had pin pricks of hot light in their very centre.

If he had been afraid of what he was going to say, what words he would somehow stumble out, John realised at once that there was no need, because what he thought of the crystal was of neither interest nor consequence to Father Ryan. This was all his. He possessed it, he loved it. No one else's opinion, praise or distaste, mattered.

He went upstairs to his room, shocked by what he had seen, and filled with a sort of horror that it was downstairs, its glitter concealed in the darkness as a flaunted sin might be temporarily hidden. But still there, still there. He lit a cigarette and opened his window onto coolness and the amber glow from the lights on the main road and again, as when he had arrived, a miasma of unhappiness and a sort of despair drifted down and settled on his shoulders.

* * *

The next months were saved for him by the people, he was welcomed and befriended, as the priests always were, though accorded respect too, which embarrassed him. 'It is the office of priest,' he said to himself, repeating the lesson learned over and again in the seminary, 'it is the office, not the man.' Though it seemed to him that Father Ryan took the respect for himself.

He was invited to breakfast and tea, weddings and wakes, and at the school the children crowded round him with eager, innocent faces he loved at once. If it had not been for all of this, every day there might be his last, he would have run away or taken a bottle and drunk himself to death.

The place was ugly and there was no escape from the ugliness. On his day off he tried to find a green blade but there was none except a small square of park with roads on either side. He went into the city and left again almost at once, fearing the concrete buildings would fall and crush him.

But all of it he might have borne, if Father Ryan had not clearly despised him.

They sat at the table in silence, except for the chink of a knife on a plate and the sound of Father Ryan's slovenly eating. He slurped and shovelled food into his mouth so that John learned to keep his eyes on his plate and wished he could put his fingers in his ears.

He missed his family with a missing that was a permanent hunger inside him, more so because he had not felt the same way during his time in the Seminary, though he had occasionally been homesick. Their letters came, though only Eileen, even with her four children now, wrote to him regularly. And Clare, who wrote twice a week, long, cheerful letters full of chat and jokes and affection.

'Remember where you belong now,' Father Ryan said. That morning's letter from her was on the breakfast table

'Too many old ties have a way of pulling you back from your duty.'

John pulled the envelope closer to him, for sudden fear that it might be confiscated, though the other priest would have no right to do that.

'It's one of my sisters, that's all.'

'One letter a month from home should suffice.'

In the seminary they were allowed that. But this was not the seminary.

'Perhaps you should think of having a word when you write next.'

'I think I won't do that.'

Father Ryan's face tautened and the small eyes seemed smaller.

'Do I have to remind you …'

'No, Father. I'm sorry.'

'I'd be obliged if you could take all the school catechism lessons tomorrow. I have appointments.'

Tomorrow was Thursday. His day off.

'Yes Father.'

He refilled his tea cup and reached in his pocket.

'That reminds me I have to ask you not to smoke your cigarettes in the house. How you find the money is beyond me and perhaps you should think of that too – but it is the offensiveness of it.'

'Am I not to smoke in my own room?'

'I would be obliged. Mrs Holmes has mentioned it to me.'

John did not believe that.

'May I have a cigarette in the garden?'

'If you must.'

He must. He went outside now and stood at the far end by the fence and the flowerless bushes and did not know how to quench the rage in him. He had never felt its like because nothing had ever prompted it but now it felt wedged in his chest and burning.

It was not having to spend his free day at the school that he minded, for he had precious little else to do. Father Ryan had a car but John did not, nor could he drive, though if the use of it had been offered he would like to learn. But it was not.

The children calmed him. He loved to be with them,

to teach them, hear what they had to tell him, to answer their questions. He could smoke in the staff room because the teachers all did and he was brought coffee and tea and biscuits. He wondered if he should have been a teacher not a priest but his vocation was still alive and he leaned on it.

There was a letter in his mother's hand on the hall table and he took it into the garden, though there was a drizzle and he had to read and smoke his cigarette sheltering against the fence as best he could.

'Bernadette's little Dominic is to be baptised in two weeks' time. If you could come home to do that it would mean such a lot, John. He is a good, quiet baby, quite large and fair-haired. Perhaps you might get just a couple of days off, though I know what life is like for you.'

She did not know. How could any of them know?

The rain came on fiercely and he went indoors to read the Office sitting at his bedroom window and after that, kneel and pray for courage to make his request.

There was tomato soup and his stomach churned to hear Father Ryan's sucking it into his mouth. He could not manage much of his own and crumbled the slice of bread onto his plate.

'There's a wedding couple who want preparation, and

it seems to me you should take them. Gregory Brown and Ann Gallagher. You'll have seen them.'

He had. A pale faced girl who always wore a knitted beret, good-looking young man. They were at every mass that was said, kneeling quietly together.

'I will. Father, there's a favour I've to ask you.' He crumbled the last bit of bread and pressed it between his fingers into a damp ball.

The other priest said nothing. The housekeeper took away the soup bowls, brought in plates of fried fish and tinned green beans.

He explained about the baptism.

Father Ryan took a mouthful of fish and beans and spoke through them.

'You're not due a holiday, Father.'

'I know that.'

A half-chewed piece of green bean dropped onto the cloth.

'It's out of the question, especially at a weekend. Now, did you see the Mrs Ramsay about the school Corpus Christi procession?'

John managed to eat a few forkfuls, refused the trifle. The rain was still pouring onto the garden.

That night he woke at two and after that could not sleep. His mind seethed with sinful images. He switched on the light and read several psalms, and then some pages of his breviary, before kneeling down to pray, but the prayers were arid and lifeless. He opened the window onto the rain, lit a cigarette and blew the smoke out as far as he could, for fear that somehow Father Ryan would sense it. The glow reminded him of standing in the darkness with Cecilia, so vividly that he could all but feel the warm breath of the horse that had stood there with them. He did not think of Cecilia with any longing or stirrings of the flesh, only with sadness.

The lights from the concrete city glowed in the distance. He lit another cigarette.

The next moments were very clear in his mind, both immediately afterwards and for years to come. People talked of confusion and a brain storm, of panic and an aberration which was unexplained and might never be recalled, but he knew none of that was true. What occurred to him was sudden and unplanned, unexpected though not unwanted, but all the time he was perfectly lucid.

He had not realised the depth of his own despair and misery, the longing to be away from this place which was worse than hunger, the need to be home worse than thirst. The unhappiness and the craving were in his bones, his spirit was possessed by them and by nothing else.

He packed methodically and quietly, made his bed and straightened the curtain.

When he opened his door, he could hear thundering snores from Father Ryan's large room at the front.

It seemed a madness to him now that he had stayed here as long as he had, and borne everything without protest, because he had felt it was a matter of obedience and he had made his vows. But he had not promised to obey Father Ryan.

He carried his case down the stairs and set it in the hall but still there was some restlessness in him, something unfinished and he cast about for the reason, standing very still. It was twenty minutes to three.

He slipped the chain carefully. Opened the door. The rain had ceased and for the first time since coming here he smelled greenness, even it was only from the wet garden.

A car went by on the main road. Quiet again. He knew what he was doing and that it was not an impulse. His head was clear, he was calm and he looked forward without being troubled.

The porcine sounds still echoed through the house. He went softly into the kitchen and beyond, to the outhouse where the tools were kept. The hammer and axe were hanging from pieces of hairy string.

When he switched on the lights briefly, to get his

bearings, the wall of crystal glittered like the jewels inside the cave of some fairy story. He looked at it piece by piece with loathing, then picked out one object, a huge glass punch bowl, its set of cups set all round on crystal hooks. He lifted it carefully and carried it outside, set it down on the flow wall beside the path.

It took more effort than he had expected, he had to swing the hammer and bring it down hard several times but then the crystal smashed and splintered and fell to pieces, the shards scattering all round.

Surely now, not only the priest inside but the next door neighbours and half the street would wake and come running. But no one did. An army of men could have robbed the house and done so undisturbed.

He picked up his case and walked in the quiet darkness towards the main road. Behind him, the mess of crystal glittered faintly in the light of the street lamp.

There would be people coming for him at the bus station or they would board the train to find him, but none did, not for the entire journey did anyone give him a glance of interest. The ferry was only half full, the crossing choppy but he stood on deck for most of the way, looking at the churning sea and waiting for the hand on his shoulder that did not come. He did not allow himself to feel his own happiness but he knew that it was there, just below the surface of his very skin, happiness and the sense of freedom. He read his Office and prayed, too, prayers that came more easily than any he had spoken for years. None of it had to do with a loss of faith or trust in God.

He had no idea what might happen but by the end of the long journey, he was too tired to think about it. He took a taxi the last miles. It was mild and still and he wound down the window to catch the smell of the air, the smell he had dreamed about. Strangely, it did not seem special now, it was the ordinary smell of evening anywhere, the same even as in the garden of the presbytery where he had stood by the fence smoking.

Nobody knew that he was coming. He met people in the street and they waved and spoke but naturally assumed that he was home on holiday and did not glance at him twice.

And then he was walking into the house.

What had he expected? When his mother had got over the surprise she was full of welcome, full of delight, sitting him down, fussing about him, making the usual great pot of tea. Joe would not be home for an hour or more.

He drank his first cup hot enough to scald his mouth and then he told her.

And after that, everything changed, as he might have

known that it would. If he had not pushed the thought away. He knew full well what he had done to her, destroyed her pride in him and her satisfaction, taken away the one thing that gave her status. 'My son, the priest.' Nothing could be the same now.

She sat with her handkerchief to her mouth, tears in her eyes but not yet falling, shaking her head every few moments.

'I'm sorry,' John said. 'I'm sorry. But if you had been there. If you'd known....' He blundered on, while understanding that his words meant nothing to her. A priest was to be obedient, to go where he was sent and stay until it pleased them to move him, he was to make the best of everything without complaint because that was the very nature of the calling, as well he knew. He had failed almost at the beginning and compounded his failure with violence and by running away.

She did not look him in the face or speak to him and after a time of sitting in the terrible silence, John went out and down through the streets and in the end, came to the gate by the old paddock. The horse was no longer there so he leaned on it alone, watching the tip of his cigarette burn red in the darkness and waiting for them to come for him.

Clare understood but what could Clare do by herself in the face of the rest? But she had kind words and those helped him. The rest was for him to deal with and for a while it was terrible and worse than he could have imagined. He remembered harsh words, hard, set faces. Shame. And then it was over.

But it broke Ma's heart and she died of it the same year, the year that Clare was married and gone to America and Cecilia had a second child and Bernadette a fifth and John walked the streets and for miles into the country, wearing out his shoe leather in search of forgiveness but without knowing where to look.

READER, I MARRIED HIM

READER, I MARRIED HIM

There was nothing they did not say about me, no name I wasn't called. I was abused to my face and behind my back.

But there was truth among the lies. They said I was ambitious, hard and ruthless and would stop at nothing to get what I wanted.

They did not know what that was, of course. How could they? They thought it was simply the King, and the title, because they could never have understood my desperate need to acquire something they had always had and taken for granted, as their birthright. And that was security. Financial. Social. Domestic. Marital. Security was all I ever longed and struggled and schemed for, because since very early and forgotten childhood, I had never had it, and my deepest, my driving fear through it all was that I never would.

Security.

Did I achieve it?

If I did, it was through men, not through my own

effort. I realise now that it was always an illusion. Even after that final, dangerous, all-or-nothing throw of the dice, even when I should have felt safe at last and overwhelmingly secure, I knew at heart that I was not. Loser had lost all.

But I am running ahead. I always run ahead now.

Poverty begot the insecurity, of course, and shame came out of it all. As I grew out of childhood, which does not understand any of this, I became aware that my father was dead and now we were poor. Genteel poverty is the worst of all, because of the contrast. My mother had aspirations. She had some small talents. She could not see herself as poor. But she had to do something about it, use the small talents, and so she embroidered things, modest little nothings, cushion covers and tray cloths, and sold them at a Women's Exchange Shop. They made very little money. But if there is nothing truly shameful about doing business with a talent for something as genteel as embroidery, my mother's next attempt to make frayed ends meet was not only a financial disaster, it was a social one. My face burns, even after all these years, when I remember. We had moved into a house converted into apartments and my mother sent around cards, asking the other tenants to dine – and pay for the pleasure. Few came, the cost of the food was more than they paid. We were obliged to go and live with Aunt Bessie. She had been watching and waiting, knowing that everything would go wrong, ready to welcome us.

I loved her. She was better than a mother. She was as dear to me as any woman could be, and she never let me down, even when it was the very thing she should have done.

But even she could not get rid of the shame and insecurity.

So I went to a ball, and why else does a young woman of nineteen go to a ball but to meet a young man?

He was twenty-seven, a naval lieutenant who had his pilot's wings. He had gold epaulettes and a dashing moustache.

For my part, I had style. I always had style, with or without money. I had a way with me. I discovered that soon enough.

He danced with me. He liked me. He even kissed me. I had style. I had confidence.

I had an evening wedding, wearing white velvet, with a pearl-embroidered bodice.
I had a husband. I was secure.

Was he in love with me? Was I in love with him? I have not the slightest idea. I knew I excited him, I know that I was excited, and flattered. I knew excitement and flattery led to marriage. And I wanted marriage.

When I made those promises, I meant to keep them, I really did. I meant to try, I really did.

After all, I was secure. Why rock the boat?

But the boat was already holed below the waterline. I found that out the moment he took a bottle of gin from his suitcase on arriving at our honeymoon hotel in Virginia, where liquor was prohibited.

If poverty and shame had toughened me, I was still a little soft-centred.

Marriage to an occasionally violent drinker baked me hard.

I went on trying, all the same. I left. I returned. Tried harder. Left again. In the course of it, I discovered that I had something that could attract the attention of other men and that was my escape route.
I did not go back again.

Oh, don't look at me like that, with scorn and the advantage of hindsight; look at me and judge me from a time when women had so few options. It was much harder for us then. I was a divorced woman. I lacked security again and worse now, I lacked respectability.

So, to hang with it. I looked elsewhere, loved and was loved, seduced and betrayed. I should have been more careful of my reputation. That came to matter, years later and far more than I had bargained for, when I thought I had buried my past, and they exhumed it. Now I still believed in marriage and craved security, but I craved respectability more. So that is what I sought.

Reader, I ...

No white velvet, candle-lit church, society column report this time. A register office and a blue coat.

I had broken up his dull marriage, but did I love him?

I was very fond of Ernest. He was kind. Good company. He had a respectable history, money though not riches.

Did he love me? I think he did.

At the least we suited each other and we were content. Is that happiness?

We moved to London and up in the world. I entertained with purpose. I had style and that impressed him. I was secure and felt it, in a way I never would again. If only it had remained there.

But then, introduced by mutual friends, we met. It was a private weekend though it still felt rather awkward. Formal. I was to learn before long that that was normal. It never quite goes.

I had a bad cold.

Ernest was beside himself, as excited as a child. He revered, admired, respected – what is the exact word for the way an Englishman views royalty, especially his future monarch? All the people we had come to know were the same but I, as an American, could never fully understand, let alone feel that way. If I had I might have trodden more warily. I had been raised to respect other people's cultures but I could never believe, as I think my husband truly did, that different blood ran in his veins and in that of all royalty. And so, although naturally I was polite – I had been taught my manners – I broke protocol, I spoke before I was spoken to, said what I thought, was forthright. And it did not seem to shock him; on the contrary, he seemed to find it refreshing. The Prince liked straight talking, because he never got it.

I understood little of this at first, and later I scarcely thought about it. On that weekend ours was a casual, social encounter and, as I wrote to Aunt Bessie, it was most unlikely that we would meet him again.

I forget who it was warned me that "Royalty offers friendliness – but never friendship." They were right. I certainly saw the ruthlessness with which he could sever even a close and longstanding relationship that had become boring or that he wanted to replace with something new and more amusing. I was warned.

But you see, what came my way was so much worse.

Everything was my fault, of course, everyone knew it, everyone blamed me. No one blamed him. But I was not the one who fell in love. I did not lose all reason, control, proportion; I did not throw away everything, *everything* else for …

For?

The world well lost for love?

He never doubted it.

Lost? No. It was not lost; he gave it away, he rejected and abandoned it. He turned his back.

He abdicated.

And all for love.

He abdicated the ultimate status. He abdicated Title. Country. Friends. Family.

Respect. Reverence. Deference. Safety. Security. Security.

And all for love. Think about that.

I do, every single day, though it has become easier. For years after it happened there was no room in my head for anything else, it was so shocking. It was, it still is, unimaginable.

Yes, but he did it, and for me. If I had been ruthless then, if I had turned my back on him, if I had clung instead to the security I enjoyed with Ernest. Who was still my husband.

If. If. If.

David was cowardly about getting rid of those he no longer wanted, always making others speak, write, reject, on his behalf. If I had made my husband take every phone call and pass on the message that I would never speak to him again, what would he have thought?

What was I? Weak? Flattered?

Yes.

I did not care about the status and the deference. That is God's truth.

The title I might have had? HRH?

A little. He cared about it more.

Did I care about him? Want him?

Yes.

No.

Did I love him? Yes.

But never in the way that he loved me, obsessively, to the exclusion of everyone and everything else. He made life difficult. He thought nothing of the trouble he caused, nothing of how I had to pacify Ernest, when he turned up without notice at our flat and stayed until two in the morning. As it went on the obsession grew. He became possessive. He once said, "I want to inhabit you, have all of you," and that was terrifying.

I loved his company. We were easy together. I adored dancing with him. I was interested in what made him tick.

I was puzzled by him.

"Sometimes I think you haven't grown up where love is concerned." I wrote that to him and it was true. He never grew up. He was always a child. A boy.

I felt sorry for him – indeed, for all of his family. That is no sort of life, you know.

I am old now and David is dead. I miss him dreadfully because he became my whole life. My only life. We spent so many years together in exile, and every, every time I looked at him, I saw a man who thought the world well lost for love.

He clung to me. He followed me everywhere. He would look around a roomful of people and if he did not see me at once, there was panic in his eyes, like a child who loses sight of his mother.

He telephoned me day and night, sometimes half a dozen times. He neglected everything else for me. He filled the flat with flowers, and I love flowers. He spent his fortune on jewels for me, and I love jewels. But what are gifts? Was he trying to buy me with them? I did not love him more because I loved his flowers and his diamonds.

People who are so comprehensively in love often want to dominate and overpower, but David was far too weak a man for that. Yet out of his desperate passion, careless of everyone and everything else, he also parted me from what I knew and loved, everything familiar and dear and sure. He took the ground from under my feet, and I had not been sure of firm ground for so very long. The only thing left to me was Aunt Bessie, my link with childhood and my growing up. With America – those other worlds. David became very fond of Aunt Bessie.

What he did was the very last thing I ever wanted but no one believed me then or does so now. He was the King and greatly loved. He had the world at his feet and the people held him in their hearts and he threw it all away. He gave up the throne for me. Can you imagine how that made me feel? Yet I wonder if he had ever really wanted it. The work bored him; he hated the stuffiness and the pomp that surrounded it. He would not miss any of it.

But it never crossed his mind that when he gave it all up, he would also lose what he had always cared most about, until he met me – his family and his country. England was his home and so much besides. And knowing it, how could they have behaved as they did? They barred him from their hearts and from returning to live at home. They gave him a royal title with one hand, and refused one to me with the other, knowing that that would hurt and demean him most of all.

He loved his mother, dearly, dearly, but she never believed it. He spent his life trying to win her approval, but he never could. What he did for love of me was the hardest blow of all for her. How did I ever find myself coming between such a mother and son? How was I ever so blind and foolish as to involve myself in any of it?

His mother blamed me for everything. I was the scheming adventuress. The gold-digger. They believed I only wanted him because of what else I would get at the same time. They never understood that I wanted neither.

Be careful of what you wish for. But I was not the one who wished for it.

And love?

I came to love him because I was all he had, because he loved me, because we were trapped together, because he was a child, because he had lost everything else, because ...

Was that the right sort of love? No. Was it enough for me? No.

Ernest left because there was no other way out – Ernest, that good, loyal, loving, unimaginative, put-upon man.

The night I sat and listened to the wireless, hearing David explain that he was abdicating because he could not face being King without having the woman he loved at his side, I wept more bitterly than I had ever wept. It was the worst night of my life. I had nothing left, no husband, no home, no reputation. I had only this man who clung to me so desperately, and the hatred of half the world.

We were sent into exile and led futile lives there.

If I had known …

But in my heart, I think I had known too well. Be careful what you wish for.

Was he happy? Was I? Did we make the best of it?

Yes.

No.

Everything comes at a price, especially love.

I wore couture. Pale blue crêpe and a halo hat.

I am going out to walk in the garden with the dogs. I love their sweet, ugly, snuffling faces. They are all I have to love now and they love me in return.

If I die before them, who will love them so well? If they die before me, I will have nothing.

How little any of it seems to matter now.

Even this ... that Reader, I married him.